"He's not going to stop until he gets what he wants. Me."

"I'm not going to let that happen," Finn said.

"You can't promise something like that." Camille reached for his hand, then thought better of making contact. "I'm the one who brought the police down on him. I'm the one who stopped him from killing more women that night. My testimony is what will put him behind bars for life. You don't know how far he'll go to make me pay for what I've done, or how many people he'll hurt to get to me. You don't know him."

"I know enough. I might not have a front-row seat into the mind of a killer like the Carver, but I know how far I'll go to keep you safe." He'd do the same for any of his witnesses, but there was something about Camille that pushed him to the edge of reason. "I was assigned to protect you. No matter what happens, you'll never have to face him alone again."

THE WITNESS

NICHOLE SEVERN

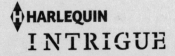

HARLEQUIN
INTRIGUE

This one is dedicated to my nanny.

She knows why.

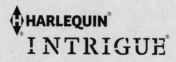

ISBN-13: 978-1-335-40155-7

The Witness

Copyright © 2021 by Natascha Jaffa

Recycling programs
for this product may
not exist in your area.

This edition published by arrangement with Harlequin Books S.A.

For questions and comments about the quality of this book, please contact us at CustomerService@Harlequin.com.

Harlequin Enterprises ULC
22 Adelaide St. West, 40th Floor
Toronto, Ontario M5H 4E3, Canada
www.Harlequin.com

Printed in U.S.A.

Nichole Severn writes explosive romantic suspense with strong heroines, heroes who dare challenge them and a hell of a lot of guns. She resides with her very supportive and patient husband, as well as her demon spawn, in Utah. When she's not writing, she's constantly injuring herself running, rock climbing, practicing yoga and snowboarding. She loves hearing from readers through her website, www.nicholesevern.com, and on Twitter, @nicholesevern.

Books by Nichole Severn

Harlequin Intrigue

A Marshal Law Novel

The Fugitive
The Witness

Blackhawk Security

Rules in Blackmail
Rules in Rescue
Rules in Deceit
Rules in Defiance
Caught in the Crossfire
The Line of Duty

Midnight Abduction

Visit the Author Profile page at Harlequin.com.

CAST OF CHARACTERS

Finnick Reed—A former combat medic, this deputy US marshal will do anything to keep his witness alive as the serial killer who attacked her tries to finish what he started, but keeping his interest in Camille professional is proving to be the hardest assignment of Finn's career.

Camille Goodman—Discovering her former fiancé was a killer all along is enough to keep her on the edge of caution. But now that she's become the centerpiece of a twisted mind game while in witness protection, the only one standing between Camille and certain death is the deputy marshal determined to keep her at arm's length.

Jonah Watson—Fellow deputy US marshal assigned out of Finn's district office.

Jeff Burnes—aka the Carver. Camille's ex-fiancé is a Chicago-based serial killer awaiting his trial date, and he's not finished with the only victim who managed to escape his blade: Camille.

Remington "Remi" Barton—Chief deputy US marshal in the Oregon district, and Finn's superior.

Chapter One

Pineapples.

Deputy United States Marshal Finnick Reed shoved his SUV into Park, cut the engine and hit the pavement of the house's driveway. Unholstering his weapon, he kept low as he approached the lakeside home from the south. He scanned what he could see of the property, the soft lapping of water at the shore loud in his ears. The sun had dipped below the horizon hours ago. Shadows shifted as spears of moonlight filtered through the ring of trees that surrounded the property. His heart pounded at the base of his skull. No other vehicles. No lights on inside the house. Everything was exactly as it should have been. Aside from the single word he and the only surviving witness of Chicago's most notorious serial killer had agreed to use in case of emergency that'd been sent less than twenty minutes ago. *Pineapples.*

She wouldn't have messaged him if she hadn't

needed him. She knew better than to put herself at risk after all these months. Finn closed in on the front door of the rambler-style river house, pressing his shoulder into the frame before testing the handle.

The door swung open without his help.

Warning prickled at the back of his neck as he stepped over the threshold. His own shallow breathing cut through the silence, and he raised his weapon shoulder level. Heel-toeing through the small entryway, he kept his boots from echoing off the hardwood, then swung into the open-concept kitchen and living area. Faint hints of light penetrated through the bay windows along the opposite wall, casting shadows through the slats of the dining-room chairs onto the floor, and Finn reached over to flip on the overhead light.

No power.

"Where are you, Red?" Camille Goodman, formerly Camille Jensen, had relocated to the sleepy coastal town of Florence, Oregon, with the help of the United States Marshals Service a year ago. As long as her attacker was awaiting trial for the murders of the six women he'd bound, strangled and carved up with his knife back in Chicago, she was Finn's responsibility. And he wasn't going anywhere until he found her. He moved deeper into the house, the slight hint of lavender in the air. Camille. She'd always had a soothing quality about her that he couldn't seem to fight, but her text message brought him to the exact opposite of calm.

She was supposed to be safe here. Protected.

He'd never forgive himself if something happened to her.

He took another step. The crunching of glass filled his ears, a hard edge of something embedding in his boot. Peeling his foot away, he recognized the phone he'd given her to contact him when she'd first been transferred into his custody. Left in the center of the living room. Dropped during a hasty escape?

Shuffling drew his attention down the hall, toward the bedrooms at the back of the house, and Finn swept his arms in that direction and took aim. He followed the sound past a room filled with large flat boxes and frames. Clear. The bathroom door had been shut, and he twisted the knob and pushed inside. Nothing. There was only one more room left in the hall. Camille's bedroom. She had to be there.

Dark spots peppered the hardwood in front of the closed bedroom door, and ice crept up Finn's neck. He slowly reached down to test the texture, but what he thought was blood shifted under his touch. His gut clenched. Red rose petals. Exactly like the ones recovered from each crime scene left behind by the Carver when he'd finished with his victims. "Camille!"

He shot upright, hauling the heel of his boot into

the space next the doorknob. The door slammed back into the wall behind it as he rushed inside. The shadowed outline of a masked intruder blurred in his vision a split second before the bastard rammed him back out into the hallway. Finn caught a mere glimpse of a pair of bare feet—motionless—as he hit the wall. Air whooshed from his lungs. The attacker went for Finn's gun, twisting the barrel down until the SOB ripped the weapon from his hand. The gun slid across the floorboards toward the other end of the hallway. Out of sight.

A fist landed a hard right hook into his jaw. Lightning flashed before his eyes as another gloved fist catapulted toward him. Finn threw out his forearm, blocking the shot, then knocked the attacker back and kicked out. His heel connected with solid muscle, but it didn't slow the masked intruder long. Finn ducked as the assailant lunged, but the man's shoulder smashed into the softest part of his gut. Pain exploded through his major organs, and a groan tore from his chest. He slammed his elbow into the base of the guy's skull. Once. Twice. The grip around the back of his thighs loosened, and Finn hauled his knee directly into the attacker's face.

The man collapsed at his feet.

Fighting to catch his breath, Finn swiped at the blood dripping from his mouth and nose, then leveraged both palms on his knees to process what the hell had just happened. Son of a bitch. Someone had broken into her house. Someone had come for her. Damn it. Pulling a set of cuffs from his belt, he secured the perp's wrists behind his back. Whoever he was, Finn would make sure the man in the mask paid for coming here tonight. He stumbled over the unconscious body at his feet and latched onto the door frame to pull himself into the bedroom. "Camille."

She wasn't moving.

He collapsed to his knees beside her. Red hair spilled out all around her as Finn lowered his ear to her mouth. Wrists and ankles bound together, she was lying unconscious between the side of her bed and the wall. She wasn't breathing, but her pulse still beat faintly against his fingers at the column of her throat. Setting his clasped hands below her sternum, he had to ignore the patches of blood across her T-shirt and count off chest compressions. Camille's blood. Get her conscious, then worry about any other injuries. He rocked forward on his knees to blow oxygen into her lungs. Her chest rose with the added air he'd given her, but even after two rounds she still couldn't breathe on her own. "Come on, Red. You're not getting away from me that easily."

Her gasp pierced through the pounding in his head. Her back arched off the floor, and his heart rocketed into his throat. Finn threaded his hand under her lower back and pulled her into his chest.

Pulling a blade from his ankle holster, he cut through the binds behind her back. He brushed her hair out of her face for the smallest chance of glimpsing those incredible aquamarine eyes. "Guess there is something to this third-time's-the-charm philosophy after all."

Her coughing jolted through him, and his insides jerked with each wheeze. Long fingers clutched onto his arm. Her soft frame molded against him as he instinctually wrapped his arms around her. At barely five foot five, Camille Goodman had fought off a serial killer who'd been a hell of a lot closer than she'd realized. Now, exactly a year later, someone else had come for her while Jeff Burnes, also known as the Carver, was awaiting trial. Finn studied the crisp lines of blood surfacing across her chest as Camille struggled to take a full breath. Red splotches spread around the collar of her shirt. The SOB had bound and strangled her, then cut into that sacred stretch of skin above her left breast to etch his claim on his victim.

The exact MO of the Carver.

How was that possible? The details of the FBI's ongoing serial case in Chicago hadn't been released, to prevent copycats from falsely taking up the killer's moniker. And Jeff Burnes's communications and visitor logs were monitored 24/7. There was no way he could've contacted anyone to get to Camille. The date, the victim—it was all too much of a coincidence. How the hell had the bastard gotten an accomplice to finish what he'd started all those months ago? The USMS had the most secure database in the country, not to mention that all records of her previous identity had been wiped completely. How had her attacker located Camille at all? "Take it easy. I've got you."

"Finn." Not "Marshal Reed." His name barely made it past her lips with the amount of damage beneath the thin skin of her throat, and rage coiled tight in his gut. She'd already been through so much since the attack in Chicago, already given up an entire life in order to stay off the Carver's radar. How much more was she expected to survive before she broke completely? Images of her leaving the hospital after the attack, of being forced to face the media as she recounted every painful and panicked moment of the attack, flooded to the front of his mind. She hadn't been handed off to the US Marshals Service at that point, but even then his protective instincts had pushed him to put himself between her and her would-be killer.

"Try not to talk until someone can look at your throat. I'm going to get you out of here." Finn forced the pain in his midsection to the back of his mind as he swept Camille into his arms. He needed to get her to safety. Then deal with the masked intruder who'd attacked her.

But when he rounded back into the hallway with Camille in his arms, it was empty.

No sign of the man who'd attacked her. No movement from the shadows.

The suspect couldn't have gotten far with his hands cuffed behind his back. Shock tightened the tendons between Finn's neck and shoulders as battle-ready tension took hold, but he couldn't stop. Not until he got Camille out of the house and called in backup. Someone had targeted her, tried to finish the job the Carver had started. He'd been assigned to protect her. She was the only one that mattered. His boots echoed off the hardwood as he carried her down the hall, and he slowed. Hell, the bastard had taken his gun. Calling that into the chief deputy would be fun in and of itself. "I don't know about you, but I think I'm killing it with this witness-protection gig. Lost my gun and the bad guy all in one night."

"My hero." Those mesmerizing blue-green eyes locked on him, and every cell in his body spiked with awareness. Thick eyebrows that matched the color of her hair stood out from creamy pale skin, and there was a hint of freckles across the bridge of her nose. Long lashes dusted the tops of her cheeks and left behind dark streaks under her eyes. From the large red markings around her neck to the color of her darkly painted toenails, he cataloged every aspect of her appearance in order to keep the details straight for the report.

Strained coughing brushed all that long red hair against his arm. The patterns of blood beneath her T-shirt had spread, and Finn picked up the pace. He'd had enough training as a combat medic in the army to know her wounds weren't severe, but the thought of her in pain pushed him to the edge of reason. He retraced his steps back through the house until cool air cleared her lavender scent from his system. Although, given how close he'd come to losing his witness tonight, he wasn't sure that was possible.

Movement registered from the tree line thirty yards across the property, hiking his pulse into overdrive. The shadows somehow seemed thicker than they had before he'd gone inside, as though there was something beyond the trees his eyes couldn't lock onto. Or someone. Finn rounded to the passenger side of the SUV, settled Camille in her seat and pulled his loaded backup weapon from the center console.

"It's him, Finn." Strain was evident in her words. She closed her eyes, tilting her head back against the seat as though intending to fall asleep. "He wants to finish what he started."

Turning away from the invisible threat, he strapped the seat belt across her midsection. Her T-shirt peeled from her bloodied skin at the collar and revealed deep, straight gouges carved into the puckered scar-ring from that first attack a year ago. Hell. "Then he'll have to come through me."

VALENTINE'S DAY.

She could still feel the tip of the blade cutting into her from a year ago, taste the betrayal on her tongue. One minute they'd been having dinner to-gether, and the next she'd fallen back in her chair as he'd lunged at her from across the table, his hands around her throat.

Just as—she'd come to learn—he'd done to so many other women.

Camille Jensen didn't exist anymore. She was Camille Goodman now. She'd worked so hard, left behind everything she'd ever cared about after Jeff Burnes's arrest, cut herself off from everyone she'd loved. He wasn't supposed to be able to find her.

The edge of the office chair bit into the backs of her thighs as she clutched the ice pack to her throat. The swelling had gone down some, but experi-ence said it'd be a few more days of rawness and at least two weeks of dark bruising before the muscles stopped hurting. Ringing phones, low conversations and whirling printers cut through the walls of glass as she waited in the conference room. The Oregon district office of the United States Marshals Service had gone on full alert, and in the center of it all was the deputy who'd been assigned as her point of contact while she'd been in witness protection.

Finnick Reed.

If it hadn't been for the marshal responding to her rushed text message before she'd secured herself inside her bedroom, she wouldn't be here.

She watched him through the glass as he spoke with another deputy on his team. Bulky veins threatened to break free from beneath the thin skin of his forearms, while those mountainous shoulders and that chest stretched his T-shirt almost to a tearing point. She hadn't been able to focus on the design across his chest when he'd whisked her out of the house, but now the white star surrounded by red, white and blue circles made sense. It was the shield of one of his favorite superheroes. Fitting, considering he'd become somewhat of a hero for saving her life tonight. Styled dark brown hair matched the thick growth along his jawline, but it was those piercing blue eyes—the ones she'd locked on the moment she'd gained consciousness after the attack—she couldn't seem to detach herself from.

His attention shifted over his teammate's shoulder. To her. Her heart rate hiked into dangerous territory. Wedging her bare feet into the industrial carpet, Camille forced herself to focus on her name written on the tab of a file folder on the shiny surface of the table in front of her. But it was in vain. The single glass door leading into the conference room opened, and her internal body temperature spiked. She didn't have to look up to know who'd come through the door. She'd become finely tuned to him over the past twelve months.

"Thought you could use a glass of water." Finn placed a small plastic-dipped cup, the kind that came stocked with office water dispensers, in front of her and took a seat at the head of the large conference-room table.

"Thank you." Two words at a time. That was all she'd been able to manage since he'd brought her here to his office in Portland before the pain flared. She wrapped shaking, blood-crusted fingers around the cup, the edges nearly folding in on themselves when she raised the brim to her mouth. Cool water soothed the stinging along the sides of her throat, but it'd take a lot more than a cup of water to help her recover from tonight. "For this. And earlier."

"I'm just glad I didn't misinterpret your SOS message for a grocery list." His lips curled up, and warmth flooded through her. She couldn't help but lock onto his face with everything she had left before the smile drained from his expression. She just needed a glimpse of something outside of the nightmare closing in. He dropped his gaze to the file in front of her, the one she was sure documented every moment of her life, starting with the attack she'd survived in Chicago and ending right here, and something in her chest tightened. Marshal Reed—Finn—interlocked his fingers on the reflective surface of the table and slid his elbows forward. He pointed to the folder with her name clearly labeled with both index fingers. "Earlier you told me 'it's him.' That he'd come back to finish what he'd started. Tell me what you meant by that."

"I…" She hadn't realized she'd said those words aloud. Dread skittered up her spine as she realized the light conversation between them had run its course, and suddenly she was back in that interrogation room in Chicago. Answering questions as to how she hadn't noticed the man she'd been sleeping with—been engaged to marry—had spent his nights killing women rather than working, as he'd claimed. Camille had known this part was coming. The marshals needed a full account of what had happened tonight. Otherwise, Finn wouldn't have brought her here after the emergency-room staff had dressed the new gouges on her chest. They'd had to leave the blood on her hands for the forensic tech to collect. Evidence.

She couldn't deny there were similarities between what'd happened a year ago and tonight. Though the haze of nearly dying in a house that didn't belong to her hadn't completely lifted yet. This didn't make sense. Jeff Burnes couldn't have been the one in her house tonight. The only reason she'd escaped to Florence, changed her name, resigned from the job she'd worked her entire life for and left her friends and family was because he was still awaiting trial. Shivers snaked down her arms, and she swallowed to lubricate her throat before answering.

"I can't explain it. Other than it felt like him. I know that doesn't count as evidence, but when he…" Her lungs threatened to spasm at the memory of those large hands around her neck. She closed her eyes, shaking her head as if that was all she had to do to forget someone had tried to kill her a second time. She'd barely survived the first attack, and it'd cost her everything. How was she supposed to do it all over again? "When I looked into his eyes beneath the mask, it felt like him."

"You mean the Carver," he said.

Every muscle across her shoulders bunched when he said the moniker the media had given the man she'd intended on spending the rest of her life with. The fresh cuts on the left side of her chest constricted, and Camille battled the urge to wrap her arms around herself. "I didn't know what he was doing."

"I'm sorry. I didn't mean… I can't imagine how difficult this must be for you after everything you've already been through, but the more you can tell me about this attack, the faster we can catch the guy who tried to kill you tonight," he said. "I can protect you from it happening again, but I need all the facts. Even the smallest detail can make a difference in us finding the man who broke into your house."

But it wasn't her house. This wasn't her life.

Finn ran a hand through his hair, then leaned back in the chair, taking the remnants of heat she'd been holding on to since she'd realized he'd been the one who'd brought her back to life. "Camille, I need to know if you broke protocol, if you reached out to someone. Anyone from your old life, any acquaintances from work. Did you log on to an old social-media account or your email?"

"The marshals monitor those accounts. You know I didn't." Her stomach soured at the idea that she'd made a mistake, that she'd brought this on herself, but it wasn't possible. She'd followed every rule, every guideline he'd handed down to her the day she'd been transferred into his protection. She'd given up a piece of herself for the sake of survival, and it'd all been for nothing. The Carver had still found her. He'd sent someone to finish what he'd started, sent them to carve the rest of his claiming mark into her chest and complete his sick ritual. Who else would've known exactly how he'd killed his victims? That information wasn't available to the public. Bile clawed up her esophagus as she picked at one corner of fresh gauze, and her eyes burned with tears. Anger mixed with fear in a nauseating combination, which only made the pain in her throat worse. "I don't know why this is happening again. I don't know who my attacker was or how he found me, and I don't know how he got inside my house—the safe house. So if you don't have any other questions, I'd like to go now."

But the thought of walking back into that big empty house, alone, only made the knot in her chest larger. She was scared. Didn't he understand that?

"Camille." Her name, said so deliberately reverent, kept her anchored in the moment. "I have every officer, including the chief of police, combing through the scene for evidence. Sooner or later, we're going to catch this guy and find out what connection he has to the Car—to your ex… But until we do, you can't go home. It's not safe there."

Safe. She studied the patches of dried blood—her blood—on her hands and slipped them beneath the table. Out of sight. It'd been a long time since she'd felt anything close to safe. The FBI's case in Chicago was stronger with the help of her testimony, but as long as there was a chance Jeff Burnes could be released, she wasn't entirely sure she understood the meaning of the word. "Where am I supposed to go?"

Blue eyes quieted the hard pounding of blood behind her ears the longer he leveled his attention on her. "We're working on that—"

Three taps on the glass ripped her back into reality, and she looked up to see the deputy Finn had been talking to earlier at the door. Behind him, chaos had overtaken the main office space as other marshals and law-enforcement officers loaded fresh magazines into their weapons and fit themselves with Kevlar. The deputy waved Finn out of the conference room, and the marshal sitting across from her stood to leave. The second deputy spoke once Finn was on the other side of the glass, but Camille couldn't hear the conversation over the soft ringing in her ears. Had the officers at her home already found evidence? Had they made an ID on the intruder? Finn snapped his gaze to the deputy before drawing his replacement weapon from the shoulder holster.

Warning pressurized behind her sternum, and she stood.

Something had happened.

He barged back into the conference room, threading his free hand between her ribs and elbow in order to wrap his arm around her. The scents of clean laundry and citrus dove deep into her lungs as he dragged her to his side. "We're leaving. Now."

"What's going on?" Ice-cold fear worked through her as he walked her back through the Oregon district office in a rush.

"We reached out to the federal team assigned to the Carver's investigation to update them on your attack tonight. In return, they told us your ex-fiancé escaped federal custody three days ago." Swinging her around to face him at the elevators, Finn released his hold on her to check the ammunition in his weapon. He pulled back on the slide and loaded a round into the chamber. He hit the button beside the elevator before turning that piercing gaze on her. "The only thing the Carver left behind in his cell was a photo of you."

Chapter Two

The FBI had kept a vital piece of intel concerning his witness to themselves in the name of avoiding a mass panic. Hell, more like avoiding having to answer for losing one of the country's most violent and deceptive serial killers of the past decade.

Jeff Burnes—the Carver—had bound, strangled and carved up six women from the Chicago area with the same word gouged into their chests. *Mine.* Six women that they knew of. Only the last person the killer had expected to fight back had been the one right in front of him.

Camille. The bastard's own fiancée.

And it looked like her former fiancé wasn't taking the hint their relationship had ended the moment he'd attacked her that Valentine's Day evening.

Finn kept his gaze on the road ahead, not on the woman who hadn't said a word since they'd left the district office. But he couldn't ignore the slight curve of her shoulders inward, or the fact she'd been picking at the dried blood on her hands since she'd gotten in the SUV. Oncoming headlights reflected off rain pattering against the windshield as he took the shortest route to get her out of downtown Portland. How the hell was he supposed to keep Camille safe if he didn't have all the information to do so? Jeff Burnes had faked a medical emergency, attacked the guard escorting him to the infirmary and stolen his clothes, and no one had noticed until it'd been too late. What'd started as a countdown until the SOB's trial date had officially become a manhunt. Marshals, the FBI, local police and every law-enforcement officer in the country had a recent photo of the Carver on their phones, and orders to apprehend, but none of that had done a damn bit of good for Camille tonight. The timing of the killer's escape couldn't be a coincidence. Three days. That was long enough for Jeff Burnes to make his way across the country and exact his revenge on the woman he'd manipulated, but the Carver wouldn't have been able to locate his only surviving victim on his own. He'd had help. "If you're not trying to make a new and terrifying fashion statement, there are wet wipes in the glovebox."

Camille leaned forward, extracting the thin package, and pulled a single wipe free. A hint of her signature lavender scent filled the SUV's interior as she meticulously cleaned her hands, and Finn breathed as much of it in as he could handle.

He'd almost been too late. Almost lost her. He'd done the witness-protection gig before in his ten years as a marshal, but he couldn't think of a single witness who'd compared to the woman beside him. Two attacks, an entire life ripped out from under her, a serial killer on her trail. Still, he hadn't ever seen her break. He'd known deputies who couldn't hold themselves together in the line of duty that long, but Camille could only take so much stress and trauma before the cracks began to show. It was his job to be there for her when they did. "We're here."

He angled the SUV into a short alleyway between a dry cleaner and a mechanic shop on the outskirts of Portland. Motion-sensor lights lit up at their approach, highlighting the wild red color of her hair. Shoving the vehicle into Park, he studied the two-story brick building for signs of movement. Dust-caked windows lined the massive rolltop door leading into the abandoned garage on the lower level, but there was no sign of any light from inside. Finn reached back into the second row of seats for the overnight bag he kept on hand, his chest brushing against her arm. Instant heat speared through him, and he gripped the bag's handle tighter than necessary to counter the effect. As much as he'd enjoyed the rush of endorphins, he had to focus on the job:

keeping her alive. After hauling the bag into his lap, Finn shouldered out of the SUV and rounded the hood to intercept Camille as she did the same.

Arms wrapped around her middle, she gazed up at the property with that legendary reserved guard in place. Fresh blood spotted near the collar of her already ruined T-shirt, and he clenched both hands into fists. Hospital staff had cleaned and glued the wound, but they must've missed a spot. She was bleeding again. She'd thanked him for saving her life tonight, but he was no damn hero. Not for her. If he had been, she wouldn't have those fresh lacerations carved into her chest for the rest of her life. "I thought you said you were taking me to a safe house. This is an old garage."

"When you have as many enemies as I do, anything can be used as a safe house." The joke was meant to loosen the hard set of her jaw, but it failed. He shouldered the duffel bag, the muscles in his midsection still sore from the fight between him and her would-be killer, and headed for the stairs leading up to the second floor. He dropped the sarcasm he'd relied on to break up the permanent tension coiling through him and adjusted his grip on the bag. "I converted it a few years ago in case I needed a place to hide. It's off the books. No attachment to the marshals or my name, completely off the grid. I already had a deputy I trust bring a bag from your house. You'll be safe here."

"The one you were talking to at the marshals office?" Bruising had already started darkening the column of her throat, shifting as she visibly swallowed. She followed close on his heels as they climbed the stairs. His awareness of her proximity was like a physical pressure between his shoulder blades.

"Jonah Watson. He's former FBI. We can trust him." Finn entered the six-digit code to unlock two separate dead bolts to the front door, and the locks retracted. She flinched in his peripheral vision, and he hesitated opening the door. He'd known this was coming. She'd held it together this long, but the barriers she'd set up to keep herself from showing emotion were starting to crumble. Trauma, terror, uncertainty. She'd lived it all in the past few hours. He faced her, discarding the bag at his feet carefully so as not to alarm her further. "Look at me, Red." Those aquamarine eyes met his gaze, and his gut clenched when the absolute determination to hold it together a little longer set into her expression. "We don't have to stay here. My job is to protect you, but if you're not sure about this or sure about me, we can go somewhere else. I can get a new detail assigned to you. Someone you're more comfortable with. I can work the case from the outside if that's what you want."

"No." Color drained from her face, almost making her skin translucent, and he had to shut down the urge to reach out for her. To put himself between her and the horrifying memories sure to haunt her for the rest of her life. Even if that was possible, he wasn't the right man for the job. He wasn't sure he ever could be as long as his own past followed on his heels. "I don't want anyone else. I trust you."

"Okay, then." He picked up the bag and pushed the door inward, trying not to let her words go to his head. She trusted him to keep her safe, and he'd do whatever it took to keep it that way. Hinges protested from the weight of the heavy steel door as they stepped over the threshold. A pool of green lighting from the emergency exit sign above gave the walls an eerie glow. Finn hit the lights along one wall and maneuvered out of her way so she could get her bearings. The space wasn't very wide. A hallway led from the entryway into a single bedroom and small bathroom at the back, but it'd be enough for the two of them until the feds caught their fugitive. He pointed to the dark duffel bag waiting on the end of the mattress. "I had Deputy Watson pack a few changes of clothes, toiletries from your bathroom and anything else he thought you might want. If you need more, just let me know. We have a set meeting location where we can hand off intel or items near here."

She moved down the hallway, each step carefully

placed along the tile as she approached the main room and stared down at the edge of the mattress. He noted the way she studied the single room, almost as though she was ensuring everything was as he said it'd be. The slim tendons between her neck and shoulders tensed as she ran her fingers over new queen-size bedding, but she didn't ask about the fact there was only one bed for both of them. She didn't have to. He'd be sleeping on the floor of the hallway with a few extra pillows and blankets he had stashed in the linen closet. Camille unzipped the bag and rifled through her things inside, then pulled away as if she'd been bitten by something.

Finn stepped to her side. "What's wrong?"

"He packed my camera," she said.

"I thought you'd like to have it considering we might be here for more than a few days." Finn slid his hands in his jeans pockets. "I know it's not the same compared to the kinds of landscapes you were used to when you worked for *Global Geographic*, but who knows. You might find something worth shooting."

He'd researched her work after she'd been put into witness protection. She was damn good. Good enough to work for the country's leading nature magazine as one of the most sought-after photographers in the industry. Her online portfolio had been filled with the enthralling landscapes of Africa, Antarctica, South America and other locations he hadn't been able to place. She'd swum with great white sharks, confronted a pack of feeding lions and hiked to the tops of mountains just for the chance to photograph an endangered species of feline that humans had never seen before. While anyone could go out and take a picture of a fox in the middle of the forest, she had the ability to give an animal a personality of its own through the way she focused on its eyes, or the angle she'd shot from. She captured impossible glimpses of what this planet was capable of with a kind of magic he hadn't seen from anyone else. For years, she'd brought a bit of wild to people's lives, a glimpse of what else was out there in the world, but now that he thought about it, he hadn't seen any new work. Not even around her home. Dread pooled at the base of his spine. Oh, hell. "Camille?"

"I haven't…" She backed away from the bag, her pulse visibly throbbing at the base of her throat. She swiped her hand beneath her nose, and everything inside of him went cold at the heartbreak etched into her expression. "My life wasn't the only thing that the Carver took from me, Marshal."

HER LIFE HAD been split into two halves: before Jeff Burnes had tried to kill her, and after.

Photography had been such a big part of her life— her passion—and being able to travel the world with *Global Geographic* had shown her things she'd never imagined possible. Waiting hours, sometimes days, in impossible conditions for a single glimpse of the most beautiful creatures and marvels this world had to offer had given her a sense of completeness and wonder. She learned patience, strength, endurance and things she hadn't believed herself capable of. She'd hiked into canyons no human had ever stepped in before in Peru, brought the world the first images of a cave beneath Heceta Head Lighthouse here in Oregon, gone scuba diving with the ocean's most dangerous predators in the Atlantic and climbed the peaks of Annapurna in Nepal. Adventure had burned in her veins and having her camera in her hand only made her experiences that much more memorable. Being behind a lens had given her purpose, given her an identity. Significance.

Until the Carver had taken that from her.

"Camille, he didn't take your life." That voice. His voice. She'd come to rely on it more than she wanted to admit over the past year—her one true connection to the outside world. The tremor in her hands settled at the sound of that rich, deep timbre, but it was only a matter of time before she broke completely. "You're still here, right now. You've survived. When this is over, you'll have the chance to start again."

Over?

"When will that be? Because from where I'm standing and the constant pain in my neck, it looks like it's just begun." Her vocal cords throbbed with every word, but it was important he understood. She centered her attention on her camera bag, which still peeked out from the duffel. "Do any of the reports in that file you have on me tell you how he and I met? That we'd been assigned to work together on an expedition the magazine was hosting for tourists to Patagonia?"

"You both worked for *Global Geographic*." He neutralized his expression, as though trying to keep the shock out of his body language, but the air between them changed. "No, none of the reports I read mentioned that."

She lifted her gaze to the marshal assigned to protect her, and an instant awareness of how close he'd gotten penetrated through the haze of anger, of shame, that'd clouded her head since that night. The muscles in the backs of her legs braced automatically, waiting for whatever came next, but he only stood his ground. Gave her the space she so desperately needed. "Photography was my life. Every time I picked up that camera, I felt as though I was doing exactly what I'd been put on this earth to do. I had the entire world available to me, and even after Jeff and I got engaged, I never planned on giving that up."

"Why did you?" he asked.

Her chest squeezed.

"The first time I unpacked my camera after the

attack, I sorted through the images on my memory card just as I've done before starting any new assignment." Gravity increased its hold on her body and took the last remaining control she'd held on to so tightly since leaving the marshals office. Camille shook her head as if the simple action could erase the memories, but of the thousands of times she'd done it before, this one wouldn't be any different. She knew that. The images were still too fresh. Too final. She had a feeling they always would be. "But Jeff had switched out my memory card with one of his own. I don't know why, but I found…"

Her breath hitched, but she forced herself to keep going in the hope that the more she talked about it, the easier it'd get.

"I found the photos he'd taken of all those women after he'd killed them. I saw their faces, their eyes." She wrapped one arm around her midsection, her hand skimming the sore skin along the base of her neck to keep herself in the moment. "It was bad enough experiencing what he was capable of firsthand, but finding out there were more victims than the FBI had identified, to see the proof hidden on my camera…" Tears burned in her eyes, blurring her vision. "I gave the memory card to the agents assigned to the case, but when I pick up my camera now, all I see is the lives he destroyed on the screen."

Silence descended between them.

"I'm sorry. I didn't realize." Finn reached for the duffel and pulled the heavy camera bag from the depths. Turning toward what she assumed was the bathroom in the corner of the room, he maneuvered around her as though if he touched her she might shatter right here in the middle of his safe house. "I can have Deputy Watson pick it up at our next exchange and take it back to your house."

"I know what you must think of me." His opinion probably didn't stray far from what she'd thought of herself for the past three hundred and sixty-five days. Camille turned to face him as he halted in the center of the room. "You think I'm letting the past control me, that I'm giving my attacker power over the rest of my life. Sad thing is, you'd be right, but I don't know how else I'm supposed to accept what happened." A burst of humorless laughter escaped from her lips and her sore throat burned. "A lot of good any of it did for me tonight."

He faced her. Brilliant blue eyes locked on her, and suddenly she felt as if Deputy Marshal Finnick Reed could see straight through her. Past the trauma, the loss of her identity, the terror. Fluorescent lighting overhead cast shadows along his angled jawline, highlighting the perfect curve of his mouth. He shifted her bag between both hands as if he was carrying a football and not one of the most important representations of her life. "I wasn't thinking of any of that."

"Were you thinking I didn't notice you've stashed a package of chocolate under the mattress?" She pointed to the corner of the bed, to the sliver of silver wrapping with the chocolate brand stamped into the foil. She couldn't hold back the smile tugging at the edge of her mouth. Because if she didn't test this connection between them, if she didn't have something outside of the sickening nightmare playing on repeat in her life to hold on to, she'd have nothing left. "I'm sure if you got ahold of their sales department, they'd tell you I'm the one keeping them in business."

"You and I would probably be tied." His eyebrows shot up as his laugh flooded through her, sank into the deep recesses she'd believed couldn't feel anymore. Finn stepped toward her, the edges of his eyes crinkling, and she fought the automatic counterstep to keep him at a distance. He wouldn't hurt her. If anything, he was probably the only person in the world who'd made her feel safe over the past year. He'd checked up on her, made sure she had everything she needed, talked with her. "This camera didn't make you who you are, Camille. What happened that night—what happened tonight—doesn't have the power to make you who you are. There's absolutely no shame in trying to find a new normal or wishing any of this hadn't happened. It's human nature. But where you see that determination to hold on to the past as a barrier preventing you from moving on, I see that it's made you strong enough to get you to this point. It's what is going to get you through the next few days, through the next minute, and is going to make sure you come out on the other side of this stronger than before."

Her mouth dried. She didn't know what to say to that, what to think. Her therapist had spent an enormous amount of time asking her to relive every detail of the attack in Chicago in the hope it'd trigger a new memory or piece of information that explained why she just couldn't accept what'd happened and learn to move on. But she already knew why. It was because no matter how many times she'd tried to deal with the anxiety, the trust issues, the constant pain of holding herself so tight all the time to get ahead of the next threat, there was a small part of her that had internalized the blame for what Jeff Burnes had done. Her FBI interrogators had gotten part of their theory right after her fiancé's arrest. If she hadn't been so focused on her career or had paid better attention to the lies Jeff had told up until that night, she couldn't help but wonder how many of those women might still be here. How many victims would never have come across his path if she'd seen the signs earlier? She hadn't strangled the life out of them or carved those four nauseating letters into their chests, but she felt just as responsible as if she had. "If you think that speech is going to stop me from getting into your chocolate stash in the middle of the night while you're sleeping, you need to come up with a better strategy."

"I'll make a deal with you." Finn moved in close, almost as if he intended to step right into her, but quickly redirected toward the bed. The comforting aroma of warm laundry surrounded her as he reached down for the silver package peeking out from beneath the mattress. He broke the bar straight down the middle, then tore open the crisp foil and offered her half. "After the night you've had, I'm willing to at least split it with you. In exchange for letting me switch out the soaked dressing on your wound."

He reached for her.

"No!" Terror dropped her body temperature, and she bolted backward until she hit the wall behind her. Panic hiked her pulse into overdrive, her lungs fighting to keep up. Bringing her hands to her shirt collar, she tried to control her breathing, but also knew Finn wouldn't hurt her. "Please, don't."

"I'm sorry. I didn't mean to scare you." He increased the space between them and set her camera and the chocolate on the bed. Dislodging the product he'd used to style his hair as he ran a hand through it, he backed off. Hands outstretched, palms forward, he nodded toward the fresh stains on her shirt—the same shirt she'd been wearing when someone had broken into her house and put his hands around her neck—and her stomach lurched. "You're just… You're bleeding through your shirt again. I have the supplies to change out the gauze, but if you'd rather do it yourself, I can walk you through it. I don't need to touch you, okay? But you should change the dressing to avoid infection."

Camille fisted her own T-shirt in her hands as a combination of shame and rage boiled hot under her skin. Her fantasy self, the one she'd built up in her head over the years and aspired to be, would be able to handle the thought of Finn touching her, of him seeing the scars—old and new—she went out of her way to hide. As one of the most confident women in the world, that delusional part of her would never let fear or trauma control her like this, but she wasn't that woman. She feared she never would be. "Can you tell me how to do it after I've had a shower?"

"Sure." He hiked a thumb over his shoulder. He picked up the chocolate bar from the bed and set it on top of the duffel his teammate had packed for her, then grabbed the bag and pushed open the bathroom door behind him. He moved the shower curtain aside and twisted the water on. In seconds, steam filled the small room, and he backed out to give her space, leaving the duffel with her things and the chocolate on the floor. "It's all yours. I'll see what I can come up with food-wise while you're cleaning up."

Her body ached as she crossed the small room toward the bathroom, an apology on the tip of her tongue. "Thank you."

Shutting the door behind her, Camille breathed heated air to battle the tenderness in her throat. Patches of red had already started to darken around her neck, distinct thumb prints visible in the oval-shaped mirror above the pedestal sink. She stripped off her shirt and the soaked gauze, forcing the last few minutes out of her mind. Swallowing a groan as the fresh gouges on the left side of her chest protested every move, she came face-to-face with the single word her would-be killer had finished carving into her skin.

Mine.

Chapter Three

He'd made a mistake.

He shouldn't have tried to touch her. The medical training that'd been drilled into him since the day he stepped into the army's ranks had made his attempt to help her so automatic, he didn't stop to think about the fact Camille might not be comfortable being touched. The carved lines in her skin had started bleeding again, and Finn had wanted nothing more than to fix the problem. That was what he did best. That was the only way he knew how to help, but it'd take more than antiseptic wipes and a fresh dressing to help Camille heal.

Deputy US Marshal Karen Reed wouldn't have made that mistake. His mother would've known exactly what to do in this situation, how to talk to a witness who'd been through the worst ordeal of her life—twice—and would've left Camille stronger than when she'd started.

Finn memorized every detail of the door separating him and the woman on the other side as shame coiled tight in his gut. He'd only managed to drive his witness away.

The constant downpour of water hitting the tiles of the shower echoed throughout the room. The existence of her camera bag seemed to pull at him from the end of the bed. Old hinges on the cabinet that'd come with the place protested as he swung one of the doors outward to get to the supplies Deputy Marshal Jonah Watson had stocked earlier. Canned beans, jars of marinara sauce, pasta, cereal, bottled water, some brownie and cake mixes, plus whatever else his teammate had stocked in the refrigerator. He and Camille would have enough food and water to get them through two or three days while the rest of the deputies in his division processed the crime scene at her house, but after the hell she'd survived, she deserved some real Oregon home cooking.

He pulled a few potatoes from the bag on the bottom shelf, along with salt, pepper and cooking oil, and set to work. Within thirty minutes, the chicken-fried steak he'd cooked up in the pan had a crisp outer layer of flour, seasoning and a mouthwatering kick of heat. Just the same as what his grandparents had him raised on.

The bathroom door clicked open, and suddenly

the heat from the pan was nothing compared to the warmth sliding along the back of his neck.

"I hope you don't mind that I borrowed one of your superhero shirts from the closet in there." Coming into his peripheral vision, she tugged at the bottom of the oversize shirt that hid any hint of the softness underneath. Her long red hair snaked trails of dampness across her shoulders as she rounded into the small kitchen and the color of her eyes intensified. "Your, uh, deputy friend forgot to pack me a clean pajama shirt and nothing else in the bag is comfortable enough to sleep in."

He strengthened his grip around the pan's handle as that lavender scent he'd equated with her hit him full force. The burn of pain cleansed the guttural urge to breathe in as much as he could, to make it part of him at the sight of her in one of his favorite shirts. He forced himself to turn back to the pan before he started burning their dinner, or managed to burn the place down, and twisted off the heat. "Not at all. Looks better on you, anyway."

"Not sure I can pull off the whole superhero thing, though, you know." Camille slid onto one of the bar stools on the other side of the kitchen counter. "They're the ones usually saving lives. Not the ones who need saving."

A new layer of emotional honesty laced her words, and the hair on the back of his neck stood on end.

True, the men and women whose emblems he wore on his shirts risked their lives to protect the world from evil, to make it a better place and fight for the weak, but they weren't always capable of doing it alone.

"Everyone needs saving at one point or another. Anyone who says different is lying to themselves." He'd learned from his own experience. His back to her, Finn removed both steaks from the pan with a spatula and arranged them on separate plates already piled with potatoes. He set one in front of her. Satisfaction coursed through him at the widening of those brilliant aquamarine eyes. "Aside from the obvious differences in choosing good over evil, there's a very thin line between a hero and a villain. A lot of times, I think it comes down to admitting you can't do everything alone, that you have to trust your team."

"Is that why every shirt you own has a superhero logo on it?" She spooned a mouthful of potatoes past perfect lips and moaned softly. "Because it reminds you you're part of the United States Marshals Service super team?"

"Uh, no. Not exactly." His laugh sounded weak, even to him, as he clenched a towel on the counter in one hand. As much as he trusted his fellow deputies to have his back on the job, that was as far as any of his relationships with them had gone. The aroma from the oil and spices he'd used on the steak battled to chase back her sweet floral scent, but in the end, he knew she'd win. She always did. He wiped at an invisible stain on the counter in order to distract himself from the question, but after everything she'd shared with him, Camille deserved to know the truth. "My mom was the first one to buy me one of these shirts. I still remember it. I was ten when she brought it home after spending two weeks on a fugitive recovery assignment down near Medford."

"Your mom is a marshal, too?" She cut through the steak with a savageness Finn imagined had been created by exhaustion, fear and draining adrenaline reserves. Some color had come back into her face, but he wasn't sure if it was from the shower, the distraction of food from her circumstances or the fact she didn't seem to be bleeding through her clothing anymore. "Sounds like your family is trying to give superheroes a run for their money."

"She was a marshal." His fingers ached from the tightness with which he held the damn kitchen towel, as though it'd take the sting out of opening up to a near stranger. Though, when he looked at her, Camille didn't feel like a stranger. Instead, there was a familiar warmth beneath all that vulnerability he hadn't felt before, struggling to break through and into the light, and some deep part of him wanted to latch onto it and hold on for dear life. "She died in the line of duty a week after my tenth birthday."

Camille hesitated to bring the fork to her mouth,

then set it back down on the edge of the plate. "I'm sorry for your loss. I can't imagine how hard that must've been for a ten-year-old. Was it hard for you after that? Did you handle it okay?"

No. He hadn't, and Finn would be damned if he had to go through that again by having someone he cared about ripped away the way his mom had been taken. He cut into his steak, but didn't raise his silverware to take a bite, no longer hungry. "I had my grandparents there to help. Good people. They took over raising me, got me through school, made sure I had clothes, food and a roof over my head until I enlisted in the army. Once you're in the military, though, your commanding officers tend to do your thinking for you, so I didn't get a whole lot of time to miss her after that."

"But now you're following in her footsteps, carrying on her legacy." Camille took on that admiring tone again, and his gut seized. The bruising around her neck had darkened over the past few hours, and her voice was still rough. As far as he could tell, the wound carved into her chest had stopped bleeding, but that didn't mean there wasn't a chance of infection. Hell, he didn't deserve her admiration, didn't deserve her secrets after nearly allowing a killer to take her life tonight. Whoever'd attacked her had almost added her name to the list of victims, and here she was looking up to him as though he was some kind reflection of the shirts he wore. Like he was some kind of damn hero. "Seems like a great way to honor her."

Sincerity laced every word, and Finn couldn't help but appreciate her attempt to soothe the hollowness he'd lived with since his mom had taken a bullet. If nearly losing his witness to a possible serial killer was honoring his mother's memory, then, yeah, he was doing a bang-up job. One thing was for sure—whether the Carver had come to finish what he'd started, or if someone else had taken up the mantle, Finn wouldn't let the bastard have a second chance at Camille. He set his plate, practically untouched, in the sink and pulled back his shoulders. "You've been through a lot. When you're finished eating, I'll walk you through how to put a fresh dressing on your wound. Then you should really get some rest."

"I haven't been able to rest for over a year know-ing I'd have to face Jeff Burnes again at his trial, and now there's a chance he was the one who almost killed me tonight." She pushed away her plate and raised her gaze to look at him through long lashes that swept across the tops of her cheeks when she blinked. "Sleep isn't going to change that."

Jeff Burnes. Not the Carver. Even after all this time, after what her former fiancé had done to her, Camille still went out of her way to humanize a man who'd taken so many lives. "I should have the preliminary report from the team processing the scene at your house by tomorrow. From there, hopefully we can get a lead on who attacked you and make some progress on getting your life back. Because sooner or later, you know the chocolate company is going to panic and call in a missing persons report on you from the dip in their sales."

"We can't let that happen." Her smile cut through the tension threatening to suffocate him from the inside, and in that moment, Finn understood exactly why the Carver had wanted to keep her for himself.

THE UNSETTLING FEELING she'd faced when she'd woken alone in an unfamiliar house all those months ago twisted in her gut.

Camille stared at the exposed wiring running the length of the ceiling above the bed. The attack. The safe house. Finn. It hadn't been a bad dream. Stinging pain demanded her attention as she shifted onto her noninjured side and disposed of the hangover of sleep faster than any amount of coffee could from her system. She hadn't expected to fall into oblivion at all. Not with a known killer out there, meticulously closing in on his prey. She propped up her elbow on the mattress and caught sight of the end of a sleeping bag peeking out from the hallway.

There was only one way in and out of this safe house, and Finn had put himself directly in the path of whoever dared to come through the front door. A combination of laundry detergent and man billowed from the shirt she wore—his shirt—and she raised the collar up over her mouth and nose to breathe a bit deeper. First resuscitating her, then fighting off her attacker, getting her to safety and making her dinner, and now physically putting himself between her and the threat that was out there, somewhere, in the real world. Was there anything Deputy US Marshal Finnick Reed couldn't do?

He'd talked of his mother as though she'd been a hero he'd looked up to, until her unexpected death when he was only ten years old, but somehow, he couldn't see that same dedication in himself. Camille could. Without him, she wouldn't have made it out of that house alive. Didn't he realize that? Her fingers automatically went to the sensitive skin of her neck.

"You're supposed to be asleep." The rough, sleep-addled filter of his voice slid through her and brushed every cell in her body into awareness. It'd been so long since she'd felt anything but fear, the jolt of concern he'd shown rocketed disquiet through her. Was he like this with everyone on his witness-protection list or did Finn consider her unique situation special? Consider her special? "Nightmares?"

She couldn't deny the sudden warmth at the thought he'd gone out of his way just for her up to this point, but Camille knew fantasy wouldn't match up with reality. It never did. The deputy was doing his job. Nothing more. Because when it came right down to it, men like him—heroes—desired a woman as impressive they were. A woman who had her life together, who knew what she wanted and went after it, and wouldn't hold back her partner. She tried swallowing around the rawness still clinging to the edges of her throat. Once upon a time, Camille might've been that woman, then her fiancé had nearly strangled the life from her. "They're not as bad as they used to be." The lie slipped past her lips easily enough. She tugged at the damp shirt plastered to her stomach. "Most nights I don't even sweat through my pajamas. Evidently not tonight."

"I'll get you another shirt." She heard rustling in the dark, then his outline solidified. He'd sat up, the weight of his gaze settling on her sternum as he shoved to his feet. The light from the emergency exit sign cast shadows across his bare back. Ridges and valleys of satisfying muscle bunched and released with his every step toward the bathroom, and the tips of her fingers tingled to test their strength. "I'll grab another bandage, too. Have to make sure your wound stays dry. Less chance of infection."

The door swung closed behind him, breaking the inexplicable paralysis running down her body. She'd be in denial if she told herself he wasn't attractive. She'd met plenty of good-looking men in her life while she'd traveled the world, but if she was being honest with herself, she'd never felt like this. Camille had never felt as cared for as she did right now. Safe. Not even in all those years she'd been with the man who'd tried to kill her.

Now she knew why.

"Lucky for you, I have an endless supply of T-shirts I never throw away." Finn wrenched open the bathroom door and flipped on the overhead light. Dressed in nothing but a light gray pair of sweats, he tossed a fresh shirt onto the bed for her. His bare feet padded across the tiles as he peeled an edge of white medical tape from the roll and tucked it underneath itself, and she couldn't help but smile at the glimpse of the relaxed, off-the-clock deputy who'd saved her life. The military and the marshals service had forged him into a masterpiece, one worth photographing for prosperity. He turned those blue eyes on her, and her heart hiked into her sore throat. After setting the new supplies on the bed beside her, he straightened, taking the tendrils of heat snaking through her with him. "You changed out the last dressing just fine. I assume you don't have a problem doing it yourself again."

Right. The bandage. Flashes of the destruction carved into her chest in the mirror's reflection arced to the front of her mind, and Camille fisted her hands in the extra shirt fabric around her middle. The nurse in the emergency room had applied a special invisible type of glue into the lacerations and closed the edges with Steri-Strips, but the letters still burned fresh. No amount of cleaning, hot water or fresh dressings would change what had been done to her, and the finality of that realization—that the Carver had returned to claim his prize—had ripped away her strength to face the result of her attack again. Shame churned hot in her gut, and she cast her attention to the supplies on the bed. "I didn't put a new one on. I couldn't…I couldn't force myself to see what he'd done."

"Oh." Finn lowered himself down onto the edge of the bed, and her center of gravity was thrown with the addition of his weight. And not just physically. Emotionally. Mentally. "That's okay. The shirt is clean and tap water is completely safe for keeping it sterile. If you don't want the dressing, you can watch out for signs of infection. Redness, swelling, pain and fever."

With the space he kept between them, it was more obvious to her in that moment that the past few hours had ripped away any kind of progress she'd made over the last year and had exposed the truth she'd tried to hide from herself and everyone around her: she didn't want to be alone. Didn't want what'd happened to define her for the rest of her life. Didn't want Finn to keep his distance. She'd spent the past year hiding in that house, too scared to face the world after Jeff Burnes had shattered it right in front of her, but she couldn't live like this forever. Always looking over her shoulder, never building any deep, meaningful connections and holding herself so tight it hurt. Her gaze lifted to the camera bag Finn had set on the kitchen counter. She couldn't have been put on this earth just to be scared. "What if I want to cover it up so I don't have to see what he carved into me?"

Finn leaned back, the medical supplies in his hand. Two notches deepened between his eyebrows, and his mouth softened at the edges. "I can help you with that."

"Okay." Her breath caught in her throat. She wasn't sure why she'd agreed so suddenly, apart from the fact he'd spent the past few hours of his life in service of her, and that something deep inside her trusted he wouldn't hurt her. Not intentionally.

"But I'm going to need you to promise that if you change your mind, you'll tell me. Anything you're not comfortable with, we stop," he said. "Agreed?"

Lungs on fire, she nodded. She didn't have the guts to look at the lacerations carved into her chest herself. This was the only way she could be sure she didn't have to constantly be reminded of that blade cutting into her and keep the wound clean at the same time. "Agreed."

"Okay." Finn shifted closer along the edge of the bed, slowly, carefully, as though he was approaching a feral animal, and her chest constricted. She didn't blame him. Not after she'd nearly put a Camille-shaped hole in the wall when he'd reached for her before, but her nerves had settled a bit more since then. Because of him. "I need a clear look at the wound to make sure there isn't anything sticking to the edges that will cause an infection."

Which meant he needed the shirt out of the way. Her body grew heavy. This wasn't about intimacy. She knew that. Finn was medically trained and was probably about as curious about her body as a gynecologist that routinely examined his patients. But the thought of him seeing exactly how much damage had been done swirled nausea in her stomach. She closed her eyes to breathe through the onslaught of self-consciousness.

"Camille, look at me. You don't have to do this. We can stop right now." Finn waited until she lifted her gaze to his, and her heart jerked behind her rib cage. The last man who'd touched her hadn't waited, and the simple consideration of consent was almost enough to break her completely.

"Yes, I do." Because she wasn't going to let her attacker win. The Carver had already taken too much. He didn't deserve her fear. She hooked her fingers beneath the collar of the shirt she'd borrowed from him and tugged it low, exposing the raw, sensitive skin where a killer had made his mark.

Finn's attention locked onto the carnage, his bottom lip parting slightly from the top one, but overall, he managed to keep his expression neutral as he tore a piece of tape from the roll in his hand. "From the look of the scarring, I'd say the first two letters were carved that night a year ago?"

"Yes." She kept her gaze on him, memorizing every detail, every change in his expression. Counting four shallow lines stretched across his forehead as he focused on her injury, she visually followed the trail to perfectly sculpted eyebrows and sideburns that grew down into a full-faced beard as a distraction from gut-wrenching exposure. She hadn't shown her scars to anyone after the night of their birth, not even the therapist she'd started seeing after she'd been relocated to Florence.

"The other two were from tonight." Not a question. "Were you conscious during…?"

"I pretended to be unconscious the first time. At least until I couldn't take the pain anymore. I think that's what surprised him the most. Jeff—the Carver—thought I was dead, that I wasn't a threat." Camille smoothed her damp palms down her thighs as the memories threatened to break free of the box she'd buried them in at the back of her mind. "He didn't plan on me fighting back."

Chapter Four

His knuckles brushed against smooth skin, but not even the fact Camille had given him permission to get this close chased back the rage spiking his body temperature higher. Finn forced himself to focus on centering a fresh piece of gauze over her wounds. It was all he could do to stop himself from calling another deputy to guard her while he joined the hunt for the bastard who'd tried to claim her as his own, who'd inflicted so much pain and misery.

Mine.

The word seemed to burn through the cotton and deep into his bones.

He'd gone over the crime-scene reports a dozen times in the past year, reviewed the photos and statements collected in the days following the attack. He'd studied the logistics of the investigation in Chicago to prepare himself for any possible scenario when she'd transferred into his protection detail, but he hadn't known the depth of her fearlessness. Until now. "I can't imagine how much strength it would've taken for you to stay still while he…cut into you."

Her chest rose on a strong inhale under his hands. A laugh escaped her lips, and he couldn't help but memorize the sound. He'd never heard her laugh before. "I'm not sure you could call what I did strength or paralysis. Either way, it gave me enough time to come up with a plan. Jeff was so focused on what he was doing…" Muscles shifted beneath the deep purple-and-blue bruising around her delicate throat, and it took everything in him not to trace the patterns with his thumb to test the sensitivity. "He didn't notice that my silverware had fallen to the floor when he'd lunged across the dining-room table for me. Once I had a steak knife in my hand, I knew the only way I was going to get out of there alive was to make sure he couldn't come after me again. So I did what I had to do."

According to the arrest reports, she'd done a hell of a job, too. Jeff Burnes—the Carver—had to be carried out of that small Chicago apartment on a stretcher from losing too much blood. Lacerated liver, punctured lung and a right kidney that couldn't be saved in surgery. The SOB was lucky he hadn't died that night.

Camille studied her hands in her lap as he secured the last piece of tape between her shoulder and sternum. "We were supposed to be celebrating Valentine's Day. Instead, I found out the man I'd planned on marrying wasn't who I thought he was."

"You lived with Jeff Burnes for years. Loved him." Those two words endangered his ability to keep up with this line of questioning, but he had to know. From the long list of women thought to be victims of the Carver over the past two years, the FBI's psychological profile theorized Jeff Burnes targeted single young women in their late twenties, sometimes early thirties, who were at the top of their career fields. A software developer, a chemist, a fashion designer, a general contractor. And the photographer sitting in front of him. There hadn't been any connection between the victims as far as the feds had been able to prove. No motive other than the sick urge to take something so beautiful and wipe it from existence. Finn leaned back, his fingertips holding the memory of how soft her skin had been to his touch. "The psychologists who've interviewed him reported he isn't emotionally capable of developing any real relationships, that his sociopathic tendencies make it impossible for him to feel love for someone else or even guilt for what he's done. Why do you think he made an effort to get so close to you? What did he want from you?"

"If there's one thing I've learned from all of this, it's that appearances can be deceiving." Her eyes raised to his, and suddenly, with the intensity in her expression, Finn couldn't remember how to breathe. "Your psychologists, the profilers, are wrong. I wish I could tell you he ticked off all the boxes of symptoms expected for sociopathic behavior while we were together, that I knew exactly what he was capable of before he attacked me that night, but I can't. He's too smart for that. Too careful."

Confusion seeped past the invisible barrier of confidence he'd built during his time with the marshals service. "What do you mean?"

"The agents who questioned me after the attack accused me of being an accessory in Jeff Burnes's crimes, of trying to cover up what he'd done because they believed I was his partner. They tried to use the memory card Jeff had planted in my camera and the fact I was the only survivor of the Carver as proof, but his fingerprints were the only ones on the card." Her knuckles fought to break through the cracked skin along the backs of her hands as she released the collar of the shirt she wore. "They couldn't understand how I hadn't noticed something off or wrong about my fiancé in all the time we were together, but the truth is, Jeff is very good at what he does."

He'd learned about the FBI's line of questioning back in Chicago when he'd first taken on her case, but even then, Finn had known they were way off base. Not a single cell in this woman's body could hurt someone. Not knowingly. "What's that?"

Other than leaving a trail of bodies wherever the bastard went.

"Manipulation. It wasn't enough for him to kill me as fast as possible. Over the past year, I realized I was something to be used, to be studied. I was nothing more to him than a toy he could disassemble and see how all my parts worked inside. He made sure to get close to me, to steer me toward relying on him, and then he learned how and when to hurt me so it'd have the most impact." Camille's tone went flat. "I don't think I was the only one. Everything Jeff Burnes has revealed to police, the FBI or your psychologists, everything he's done while he's been under surveillance in prison, is to make them believe what he wants them to believe. He wants them to think he's a sociopath because that would fit into something they're familiar with, but the truth is he's far more dangerous than you realize. He's not going to stop until he gets what he wants. Me."

"I'm not going to let that happen," he said.

He meant it. Despite the danger closing in, this was what Finn had been trained for, what he'd risk his life for. He'd become a marshal to ensure no one else had to lose a loved one to violence like he had, and he wasn't about to break that oath with Camille. She'd spent the last year of her life separate from the people she loved, alone in that big house, lying to everyone she came into contact with in an effort to survive. She deserved not to have to look over her shoulder for the rest of her life. She deserved more than this.

"You can't promise something like that." She reached for his hand, which had settled near hers, then thought better of making contact. Gaze downcast, she seemed to almost curl in on herself. She'd trusted him enough to patch her wound, and he couldn't imagine how hard it'd been for her to open up that much. The fact Camille was still sitting here, talking about that night a year ago after surviving a second attempt on her life tonight, was damn near unbelievable. "I'm the one who brought the police down on him. I'm the one who stopped him from killing more women that night. My testimony is what will put him behind bars for life. You don't know how far he'll go to make me pay for what I've done, or how many people he'll hurt to get to me. You don't know him."

"I know enough. I might not have a front-row seat into the mind of a killer like the Carver, but I know how far I'll go to keep you safe." He'd do the same for any of his witnesses, but there was something about Camille—something he didn't have the courage to consider—that pushed him to the edge of reason. Once the prosecution had Jeff Burnes behind bars for good, she'd pick up her life where it'd left off, and Finn would move onto his next assignment for the marshals service. Just as he had any number of times before. But where he'd been able to compartmentalize his past witness's faces and situations at the back of his mind after each protection detail ended, he had a feeling Camille wouldn't go quietly. "I was assigned to protect you. No matter what happens, you'll never have to face him alone again."

She rolled her lips between her teeth and nodded once, long red hair bouncing against her shoulders. Her hand drifted to her throat. "Every time I've had to tell people what happened that night, the more self-conscious and misunderstood I've felt. Like each iteration took a piece of me to the point I can't remember who I was before I met Jeff." The weight of those hypnotic aquamarine eyes increased the pressure behind his rib cage. "But when I talk to you, I don't feel lonely. I don't feel misunderstood. For the first time since that attack, I feel…like me."

He didn't know what to say to that. Didn't know what to think. He'd done what any deputy would've done in his situation, but Camille—

The sudden vibration from the phone in his pocket ripped him back to reality. Finn drove his hand into his sweats and read the name. Jonah Watson. The screen lit up as he connected the line and brought the phone to his ear. He held up one finger, asking for a minute. "Please tell me this isn't a social call."

Camille slid off the bed, the fresh shirt he'd gotten for her from the closet clutched in her hand. She headed for the bathroom. Soft hints of her lavender scent settled around him as she ducked into the small space and closed the door behind her, but somehow the tension tightening the muscles down his spine only increased.

"That depends," Deputy Jonah Watson said. "Do you consider a body a social call?"

SHE COULD STILL feel his hands on her.

Camille carefully switched out the shirt plastered to her skin for the fresh one Finn had pulled from the closet. The white patch of gauze taped above the left side of her clavicle stood stark against her skin in the mirror's reflection but provided ample coverage from the destruction underneath. Warmth clung to the oversensitive skin around the area, and she couldn't help but trace the pattern the deputy marshal had made with his fingers.

She'd been torn down to mere ashes after the attack, but when Finn had touched her a few minutes ago, when he hadn't shown disgust at the carnage carved into her chest, she'd almost believed she could rise again. That her fantasy self and real self could merge and become the whole, self-aware, creative woman she'd once been. In those short moments, she'd envisioned her art washing away the shadows of the past, and the resulting ache had embedded a desire like nothing she'd felt before. She'd prayed for so long for the strength to defeat the constant pain of fear and isolation, but for the briefest moment, she was reminded of how much she'd already survived.

Because of his confidence in her, his promises to keep her safe.

It'd been so long since she'd let herself savor the touch of another person. She'd been better off alone all these months, apart from anyone who could hurt her, but he'd made shedding her guard easy. For a series of breaths, he'd helped drain the poison of anger, betrayal and hurt from her veins. Not out of domination, as Jeff had, but concern. Respect.

The Carver. The man she'd known as Jeff Burnes hadn't really existed.

She caught sight of the camera bag Finn must've hidden on the closet shelf when she'd gone to bed. Surrounded by an entire array of superhero shirts, the black canvas seemed innocent enough in this safe haven. Victim. Witness. Target. She'd been called so many things. By the officers who'd arrived on the scene, the agents who'd interrogated her, the marshals in Chicago before she'd been relocated to Florence, Oregon. Labels had defined her for the past twelve months, but they hadn't done anything but steal her very identity right out from under her without her noticing. There had to be a point where they stopped holding so much power over her, where she could take back control of her own life.

The tense rumble of Finn's voice penetrated through the bathroom door, but the tug of something she hadn't felt in a long time surfaced the longer she studied the camera bag. Familiarity. Longing. The tip of her right index finger burned at the idea of feeling the smooth plastic of the shutter button again, and she curled her hands into fists. One step. Two. Mere inches separated her from the instrument she'd used to bring her lifelong passion to reality. Camille hovered her hand over one of the zippers that sealed her camera inside, and suddenly, the nausea hit. The memories of those photos of Jeff's victims—the muscles in her jaw hurt, the *Carver's* victims—he'd hidden inside her camera were still as clear in her mind as they'd been that day she'd discovered them.

Her finger grazed the metal zipper, and a rush of hesitation swept through her. Thousands of photographers dreamed of traveling to remote locations to learn about hidden cultures, ecosystems never seen by the human eye and documenting events inside land-mine-ridden war zones. Although wearing a giant panda suit in order to photograph a baby panda bred in captivity and scheduled to be released into the wild in China wasn't an assignment she'd expected while working for *Global Geographic*, photography—no matter the subject in her lens—had empowered her. Being behind the camera had given her the gift of emotional self-reliance in a lonely, sometimes demanding career, but the people she'd met, the experiences she'd had… They'd been everything. They'd been worth the discomfort, the sickness she'd contracted on assignment, each time she'd had to put her life in danger to get the perfect shot. How had she allowed her passion to be ripped away from her so easily?

Camille pinched the zipper between her thumb and index finger and slid the bracket around the unique curve of her camera bag. Lighting above the bathroom sink highlighted the matte polycarbonate casing. Air stuck in her throat as she curved her fingers around the padding surrounding the delicate device and peered inside.

Three soft knocks reverberated through the bathroom door.

She pulled back her hand, her heart pounding at the base of her throat, and faced the door.

"Camille?" The tension she'd heard earlier during his phone conversation vanished as Finn said her name. "I need to know you're okay."

Glancing at the open camera bag on the shelf, she forced herself to swallow the uncertainty that'd built at the back of her throat and secured the zipper back in place. She'd taken the first step to breaking through the haze that'd suffocated her passion for photography and come out on the other side no less broken. Maybe that, in and of itself, was a start. Cold bled into the center of her palm as she turned the doorknob and tugged the door open. Bright blue eyes leveled on her, and the last tendrils of her anxiety dissolved. "I'm okay."

His attention dipped to where her wound ached beneath her shirt. "If having me touch you made you uncomfortable—"

"No, it's not that." If anything, the simple act of letting him get that close had given her the strength to push at the invisible bindings that'd been keeping her from picking up her camera. With his help, she'd tested herself more in the past twelve hours than she had over the past twelve months, and there wasn't a single part of her that regretted it. Camille leaned her shoulder against the door frame, her hand raising to the puckered outline of the gauze through her shirt. "I'm the one who asked you to make it so I couldn't see the wound, and that's exactly what you did. Thank you."

His lips parted as though he needed to process what she'd said, as though he'd expected her to face him with the debilitating uneasiness she'd used as a crutch for so long, but Camille couldn't be that woman anymore. Not if she was going to get her life back. It'd take time, but just as she'd taken cover from a storm for twelve hours inside a mountain cave to catch a glimpse of the rarest cougar in the world, finding herself after trauma would be worth the risk.

"Happy to be of service." A dose of casual charm brought one corner of his mouth up into a crooked smile, and her heart thudded wildly in her chest.

"Was that your marshal friend on the phone?" Digging her fingernails into her opposite arm, Camille fought to keep the blatant admiration for her protector out of her voice. "Were they able to recover any evidence from my house or confirm that was Jeff Burnes who attacked me?"

"No. Whoever broke in and tried to kill you was careful to wear gloves and had most likely planned his way in and out ahead of time. The storm didn't help, either. Any tracks he might've left behind were washed away within a few minutes, which could be a happy coincidence or had been perfectly timed." He folded his arms over his chest, raising her awareness of the thick ropes of muscle under his shirt to a whole new level. "But the search team I had combing the woods around your house found something else. Someone else."

"Someone?" Camille was gripped by confusion. "What do you mean? You just said the marshals didn't find—"

"It's another victim, Camille." He lowered his

voice to a point where she could barely register his words through the hard pulse behind her ears. "She was dressed in running gear and tennis shoes. Florence police believe she was out for a jog on the trail that cuts through those woods when she was attacked about twenty-four hours ago."

"That doesn't…" She shook her head. It didn't make sense. A woman had been killed near her home within a few hours that Camille had been attacked? What were the odds? She cleared her throat, trying to force the words to take form, but a nonexistent earthquake rocked through her and stole the air from her lungs. No. She was getting ahead of herself. Just because the Carver may have come for her again didn't mean the cases were connected. "How did she die?"

His expression hardened, and in that moment, she knew the answer before the words left his mouth. "Bound, strangled and carved with the word *mine* above her left breast. The search team found a trail of red rose petals leading straight to the location her body was found."

The door frame wasn't enough to keep her upright.

"It's happening again." Her gut clenched. Camille stumbled back a step as the information cut through her, barely catching herself on the vanity before her legs collapsed right out from under her. She could have every intention in the world to move past the attacks, to heal, but the truth of the matter was the Carver wouldn't let her go. No matter where she ran, no matter how many times she changed her name, he would find her. He would hurt more people. He would come for her again and again until she finally lost the battle to survive.

Finn moved slowly, setting one hand beneath her elbow to help keep her on her feet, but where she'd found comfort less than ten minutes ago when he'd touched her, there was only nausea now. "I'm sorry. I wasn't sure whether or not to say anything to you about it, but you are the only woman who's survived this kind of attack. We need your help to bring this bastard down."

Her help? She could barely help herself. What on earth could she possibly do against a man determined to destroy so many lives? Camille sank to the floor, her back pressed against the vanity cabinet. "Who was she?"

"The Lane County medical examiner's office has already been able to pull prints and get an ID." Crouching in front of her, Finn took out his phone from his sweats and turned the screen to face her. A woman, maybe in her early thirties, with long red hair, freckles across her nose and dark green eyes, smiled back in what looked like a photo a loved one might hand over to law enforcement when a family member disappeared. "Her name is Jodie Adler. Do you recognize her?"

"No." But she couldn't ignore the similarities between herself and the victim found near her home. The hair, the age, the eyes. Her throat burned with awareness. Camille was going to be sick. "But I think I know why he chose her."

"So do I." Finn swiped his finger across his phone's screen, and every cell in her body prepared for the worst. "That wasn't all the medical examiner found when she started Ms. Adler's autopsy. The killer left a note in the victim's mouth after he was finished."

He offered her the phone.

She swallowed the bile working up her throat as she studied the photo of a crumpled sheet of paper with scrawling black ink. "Happy anniversary, Camille."

Chapter Five

Pain shot through his thumb as Finn ended the call with the deputy chief of the Illinois USMS division a bit harder than intended. Damn it. He'd reached out to everyone he could and had asked his own superior, Deputy Chief Remington "Remi" Barton, to do the same. So far, nobody in the marshals service, the FBI or the Illinois state police had been able to narrow down Jeff Burnes's location. Interviews with the SOB's cell mate at MCC Chicago had gotten them nowhere. Every second the Carver wasn't behind bars was another chance for him to get to Camille.

"Anything new?" Her voice remained steady, her expression soft, and an unwelcome shot of awe loosened the tightness in his chest. Not only had she trusted him to clean and patch the lacerations on her chest without giving in to her urge to pull away, but she'd also kept herself from falling off the emotional roller coaster after discovering a killer had once again put her in his sights. How the woman wasn't curled up in the bathroom in the fetal position, he didn't know, and he couldn't help but admire the display of inner strength he hadn't expected her to possess—which wasn't his job.

"Not yet." Whoever'd killed that woman near Camille's home had used the same MO as the murders in Chicago, but none of the forensics from the attack on his witness, or what had been collected from the crime scene in the woods, could verify the Carver as their suspect. Other than the addition of the note, with "Happy anniversary, Camille" written in dark ink, there was no forensic proof to definitively pinpoint that Jeff Burnes had picked up where he'd left off, and Finn couldn't do a damn thing about it as long as he was assigned to protect her. He wanted to be out there, wanted point on the investigation, so everything had to go through him. The more intel he had on his enemy, the better prepared he'd be and the sooner he'd see the threat coming, but the thought of leaving Camille in the hands of another deputy burned an ulcer into the lining of his stomach. He caught sight of the superhero logo emblazoned across the shirt he'd given her for the night. Hunting a serial killer while keeping his witness protected at the same time? No problem. If he'd been one of the damn superheroes he'd idolized most of his life. Which, despite Camille's admiration for him having saved her life, he wasn't. "Whoever attacked Jodie Adler obviously knew we'd have the woods around your house searched. He knew exactly where to leave her to ensure you'd get his message. From the note he left behind, we have to assume he's making this entire mind game about you."

Hell, if Beckett Foster—the deputy with the highest fugitive recovery rate in all of Oregon—wasn't on his honeymoon somewhere on a tropical island with his pregnant wife he'd once been assigned to bring in, Finn would've called in the marshal to aid in the hunt. But, for now, he and Camille were on their own while the rest of the marshals from his office followed leads.

"Lucky me." Her shoulders rounded inward. The whitening of Camille's knuckles against the dark ceramic mug of coffee tugged at something primal he hadn't let himself feel since he'd been ten years old.

He'd followed his own set of self-imposed rules when he'd taken that first step to following in his mother's footsteps. Emotional involvement—of any kind—only ensured pain and abandonment when the people he cared about left, or were taken from him. It was an experience he wasn't too keen on going through again, but there was something about Camille Goodman that wanted him to break that rule. He itched to pull her against him, to comfort her, to promise her she was safe as long as he was assigned as her protection, but he'd already proven that wasn't the case. Had he walked through her door thirty seconds later, Camille wouldn't be sitting here at all. She would've been taken under his watch, and there wouldn't have been anything he could do about it.

Something more than physical exhaustion deepened the color of her gaze as he studied her. She'd already been through so much—a second attack, being forced to relocate once again, learning another woman had died in her place. The sooner they caught her attacker, the sooner she could get her life back. She'd given her statement to Florence officers in the emergency room after the incident, but Finn had been busy giving his own account of what'd happened. Almost a full day had passed since then. Maybe something she hadn't thought to mention at the time could make all the difference in finding the bastard who'd come after her.

"Did he say anything to you? When he was in your house?" he asked. "When he…"

"Strangled me?" Her jaw ticked as she studied the liquid in her mug. "My therapist once told me the more times we're forced to recount a memory the human brain changes it slightly to protect itself from suffering trauma all over again, but I don't think that's true in every case. There are some things you can't forget." She lifted her gaze to his, and gravity threatened to pull him straight into those aquamarine eyes. "I remember every second of him being in my house. I remember what he smelled like, the color of his eyes, the feel of the knife cutting into me all over again. No. If he'd said something, I would've remembered."

"You were conscious when he engraved the last two letters into your chest?" The muscles down his spine hardened, drawing his shoulders back. "Were you pretending to be unconscious like you did back in Chicago?"

"I…" The edges of her eyes narrowed as her shoulders relaxed away from her ears. Confusion contorted her expression for the briefest of moments, her eyebrows drawing inward before she shook her head. Her hand seemed to float to where he'd patched the lacerations without her noticing. "No. I was running for my bedroom after sending you that message, and… Something pinched my neck. I got dizzy, and I fell. I must've blacked out because when I came around, he was sitting on my chest with his knees pinning my arms to my sides. He'd just started cutting."

"What happened when you woke up?" His heart pounded hard behind his ears.

"I tried to roll him off me, but the space between my bed and the wall was too narrow. He got his hands around my throat, but the more I fought back, the harder he squeezed, until…" She slipped off the bar stool and faced him, her mug forgotten on the counter. "I already said all of this to the officer who took my statement. You were there. Why does it matter?"

"Because he broke the pattern." Finn crossed the small space to the hallway where he'd set up his makeshift bed for the night. Grabbing his duffel bag by the handle, he tugged the canvas closer and retrieved the thick file from the bottom. The original investigation reports. Crime-scene photos, witness statements, background checks, evidence logs, autopsy reports. It was all here. Everything he'd needed to know about Camille's attacker and the victims Jeff Burnes had targeted. He flipped straight to the autopsy reports, scanning one after the other as he slowly closed the distance between him and Camille, then moved onto the next. "Every victim the Cook County medical examiner autopsied connected to the Carver's investigation was engraved with the word *mine* after he'd already strangled them. Not before."

"You brought the file here?" Her voice sounded so small then, miles different than a few minutes ago, and Finn raised his gaze in time to watch the color wash from her face. She stared at the case file in his hands, and he closed it on instinct. Hell. He hadn't been thinking about… He hadn't meant for her to have to confront these photos. Not after what she'd told him about Jeff Burnes hiding victim photos on the camera's memory card.

"When I take on a witness-protection detail, I do my homework so I'm prepared for any threat that might come out of his or her past, but I'm sorry. You weren't ever meant to see this." A sickening knot twisted in his gut. He should've had more sense than that. Should've known better. Finn turned, slid the file back into his duffel bag and zipped it shut, but that wouldn't hide the fact he'd brought it into a safe house that was supposed to be a safe space for her in the first place. Straightening, he faced her. "I wasn't thinking, and as soon as I can I'll make sure to hand it over to Deputy Marshal Watson so you won't have to see it again."

"Hiding it out of sight isn't going to make my feelings and memories about what happened go away." Soft red hair waved below one shoulder, a line of tears welling in her eyes as she smoothed her thumb over a small white wire sticking out of her sweatpants. Headphones. The heater kicked on, and an instant jolt rocked through her as though she expected the Carver to barge right through the front door.

"I know, and I'm not sure there's anything that can, but I promise to be more careful from now on." Finn kept his feet cemented in place. She'd held it together this long since the second attack, but the cracks in her outer armor were beginning to show. Combined with the pain she surely felt every time she breathed and the lack of sleep, he couldn't imagine the amount of determination, the strength, it took not to collapse back into that bed and hide. How long did she expect her body to hold up under this much stress and pressure without giving out? He'd been assigned to protect her physically until Jeff Burnes reached his trial sentencing, but that job was going to get a hell of a lot harder if his witness wasn't taking care of herself mentally and emotionally. He nodded toward the headphone wire near her left hand. "What do you listen to?"

"What?" Her lips parted a split second before she lowered her attention to the plastic casing peeking out from her pocket. Slipping her thumb along the wire, she held on to it as though it was an anchor keeping her from vanishing right off the face of the earth. "I…I listen to white noise. Usually rain, when I can't pull myself out of an anxiety attack. It helps calm me down."

Rain. Completely random and completely perfect for the woman standing in front of him. Finn took a single step, slowly, and offered his hand. Those brilliant aquamarine eyes swirled with confusion for a brief moment before understanding hit. She reached into her sweats and tugged the headphones from her pocket. Handing him an earbud, she inserted the other into her ear then pressed Play on the button below her chin. A roll of thunder gently cascaded into his left ear, followed by a constant patter of rain, and an undeniable wave of ease released the tension from around his spine. Interesting. "I like it."

"I know it's probably something your boss might discourage between her deputies and the people they're supposed to protect, and if I'm asking too much I'll understand, but I…I don't want to be alone right now." She lowered her gaze to the scrapes along the backs of her hands, then pinned him with the desperation etched into her expression. "Will you sit with me until I fall asleep?"

Air locked in his throat.

The USMS had good reason for discouraging interpersonal relationships between marshals in the same district or with assigned protective details. Giving in to personal requests breached the professional barriers set between marshals and witnesses, which led to a sense of friendship, deeper emotions and mistakes.

"I can do that." Finn understood firsthand the danger of agreeing to Camille's request, but he was already moving slowly toward the single bed with her in tow. He took possession of one side while she climbed over the mattress and lay down on the other, never once breaking their headphone connection. The bed dipped with their combined weight, pooling them in the middle as the storm in his ear lightened. Her body heat bled through her sweats into the side of his thigh after a few erratic heartbeats, but in that moment, Finn couldn't imagine himself anywhere else but right here. Protecting his witness from whatever monsters awaited her when she closed her eyes. "I'll stay as long as you need me to."

IT'D STOPPED RAINING.

Camille slipped her arm from over her eyes, her body heavy with one of the best nights of sleep she could remember. The earbud she'd fallen asleep with slipped down her neck, and a sudden awareness of how quiet it'd gotten intensified the sound of her heartbeat in her ears. Prickling needled through her shoulder as she rolled to one side and hit something solid and warm. Not something. Someone.

The drugging haze of sleep faded from her vision as she realized how close she'd gotten to him in the night. As though she'd subconsciously sought out Finn and pressed right against him in sweet oblivion.

Over the past year he'd checked in on her once a month and had run through the protocols of being in witness protection with every random visit. Had she been in contact with any of her friends and family? Had she noticed any suspicious behavior or the same car hovering around the property? With the paths of communication to her old life off-limits and out of reach, she'd started looking forward to those short meetings, the chance to get to talk to another human being where she could be…herself.

Not Camille Goodman, the newest resident in a small coastal town made up of barely 8,900 residents as a freelance virtual assistant to a handful of entrepreneurs. Not the woman who only left her house once a week for groceries and kept to herself because the rumors about who she was and where she'd come from whispered around her every time she went into town.

With him, she was Camille Jensen, born and raised in Chicago. The same Camille who'd put herself through four years at Northwestern University and worked every hour of every day to land her dream job as one of *Global Geographic*'s new wave of photographers. A traveler, sister, daughter, coworker and friend. Someone who didn't have to worry about the future or look over her shoulder for the next threat. Someone who'd lived in the moment and didn't second-guess interactions with the people around her. During those check-ins, she didn't have to lie.

She didn't dare move. Didn't dare lose this sense of connectedness to another person. Something she hadn't let herself feel in a long time. Because in those brief interactions over the past few months, talking to him—trusting him—seemed almost easy. Effortless. The ridged sweep of hair over his forehead curled down along one side of his face, softening the hard, often guarded, angles he kept in place while conscious. Cords of strength shaped impressive muscles down the arm she'd turned into during the night, his body heat tunneling through the thin fabric of her shirt. At nearly six foot four, the queen-size bed barely contained his mountainous frame, but where the men in her past life—where Jeff Burnes—had used their size to intimidate her, Finn used his size to protect. The urge to push the strand of hair away from his face tensed the muscles in her hand, but she didn't want to wake him. Not if there was a chance she could extend this moment longer, a chance to just…feel. Stillness. Peace. Quiet.

"Some people might think it's creepy when you stare at them like that." He kept his eyes closed, but the fact he hadn't slurred his speech and made sense told her he'd been awake for a while. Possibly as long as she had, and her pulse ticked up a notch. How long had he been lying there? Aware she was watching him?

"You didn't seem to mind." Sweat trickled at the base of her spine as she put a few inches of space between them. Setting her headphone cord between her thumb and index finger, she rolled the casing under her fingernail and pressed down. "You know, it's impossible to tell what time it is or what day it is without windows in this place. Like we're so far removed from reality, that nothing exists outside of these four walls. It's disconcerting and comforting at the same time."

Clear blue eyes peaked out from a thick line of

dark lashes and settled on her. "I bought and reno-vated this place when I came home from my second tour with the army. With the soundproofing and lack of windows, it gets to feeling like a sensory depri-vation tank when things get out of control. I come here between assignments sometimes to shut down, get away, but I'm still close enough in case my of-fice needs me."

"I can't imagine how hard that must've been for you, having to be a combat medic in a war zone all that time. Having to see all that hurt and pain." Maybe as hard as it'd been for her seeing all those women collected on Jeff Burnes's memory card like trophies. Or was it worse because he hadn't been able to stop the threat from taking more lives? Ca-mille let the headphone cord slip from her grasp and replaced the pressure under her fingernail with the hem of his T-shirt.

"That's part of the deal when you sign your life over to the government, but at least over there I knew who the enemy was." His attention dropped to her hand a split second before he swung his legs over the edge of the bed. He pushed to his feet, out of her reach, and in an instant, the connection she'd felt be-tween them was compromised, like a rubber band on the edge of snapping in two. With his back toward her, Finn pulled a fresh coffee mug from the single cabinet in the corner of the kitchen, emergency lighting highlighting rough ridges of puckered skin on his left shoulder blade. "Working for the marshals is a different story. The threat could come from anywhere." He filled his mug with water from the sink tap and took a gulp. "Anyone."

Camille set her bare feet on the floor, every cell in her body attuned to every cell in his. The tape he'd secured on the left side of her chest tugged at sensitive skin as she closed the distance between them. The muscles down his spine hardened vertebrae by vertebrae as though he sensed how close she'd gotten. She reached out, tracing the pattern of scar tissue puckered two inches to the left of his spine, but he didn't pull away. Didn't turn on her. His shoulders sank on a strong exhale under her touch, and she couldn't seem to force herself to stop. A gunshot wound? "I didn't know you had any scars."

"Don't we all?" His voice dropped into dangerous territory. Guttural. Pained. He faced her. So close. So real. Men like Jeff Burnes—the Carver—manipulated, hurt and betrayed the people they were supposed to care about, supposed to support and protect, but Finn wasn't like them. She saw it in the way he'd put himself between her and the man who'd attacked her last night, felt it in the way he'd ensured to keep his distance while they'd shared the bed, but more than anything it was a gut feeling. One she'd learned to trust since her fiancé had tried to kill her last Valentine's Day, and right now it was telling her that being within his arm's reach was the safest place she could be. She'd never had anyone be as gentle with her as he had. Not just with sweeping her to safety or cleaning the wound on her chest, but through the comfort he'd offered so she could get to sleep. The concern he'd shown. "My mom's last assignment as a marshal was a fugitive recovery case. A man who was sentenced to ten years for the death of his newborn. It was supposed to be routine. Nothing she hadn't done before. Routine search, upping the protection detail around his wife, who was set to testify against him, connecting with acquaintances as to where he might go. Deputy Marshal Karen Reed was the best, and she always got her fugitive."

Yet she'd been shot in the line of duty.

"What happened?" she asked.

"She still had to be a mom to a ten-year-old kid." He drove his hand into his sweats pockets, the fabric molding to the outline of the backs of his knuckles as though he'd wrapped his hand in a tight fist. "She'd leave me with my grandparents when she was on assignment, but they could barely take care of themselves, let alone me. So she'd come home when she could, no matter how many miles or how many hours it'd take her. Sometimes I'd stay awake long enough to get a glimpse of the headlights of her SUV crawl across my bedroom wall, but I'd really know it was her when she'd come to check on me. I remember she always looked so dead-tired from the long days, the long drives. So tired she hadn't noticed the man she'd been closing in on had followed her home one night."

Awareness of where they were penetrated through the engrossing intensity of the conversation, and it took every ounce of strength she had, every fiber of her being, to break through the anxiety and terror of getting close to another person to reach out for him. She set her palm over his heart. "Finn, I'm so sorry. I had no... I didn't know."

"I was pretending to be asleep when she leaned over me to kiss me good-night. Didn't even know what was happening before the bullet went straight through her and into my back. By the time I got through my own shock, it was too late for her. I couldn't do anything but watch her die right in front of me." Finn lowered his chin to his chest and slid his hand over hers, and heat unlike anything she'd felt before exploded through her. "You're right, you know. About our brains changing small details in order to cope with trauma. It's garbage. Because I remember everything about that night, too."

"Did they find him?" Camille studied her hand beneath his, memorized the feel of his heart pounding under her fingers. She raised her gaze, locking onto the crisp outline of his mouth, and suddenly she wanted to be the one to comfort him, to help him forget the nightmare of his past. "The fugitive who followed her home that night?"

"Her team caught up with him within a few hours, before he hit the Canadian border." Finn stepped away. Away from her, but she couldn't take it personally. There'd been dozens of times over the past twelve months when she couldn't stand the thought of being touched, of being vulnerable around someone else, let alone a stranger, and he deserved the right to choose for himself how much was too much. Just as he'd done for her. "Bastard shot himself in the head before they could force him to serve his time behind bars for what he'd done. He took the easy way out and left a trail of hurt and death along the way, and there's nothing that can convince me to go through that pain again."

Again? The heat left her hand the longer she stared up at him. "What do you mean? You were ten years old. You're not the one who pulled that trigger. You're not responsible—"

"If it hadn't been for me, my mother never would've been there, never would've led a killer into her home and never would've died protecting me. She got herself killed because she let her emotions get in the way of the job." Finn held the mug of water with one hand, his grip tight as he faced her. "That's why I have to make this clear to you, Camille, before you get any more ideas of me being some kind of hero or start thinking something might happen between us. Until Jeff Burnes appears for his trial date, you're my witness. Nothing more. Because I'm not willing to make the same mistake my mother did."

Chapter Six

She hadn't said a word to him for the past hour, yet his awareness of Camille had hit an all-time high. From the way she used a wall of long, red hair to block her view of him, to the fact she'd unpacked and repacked the overnight bag six times now and had changed into a shirt to replace the one she'd borrowed from him.

Finn had tried reading the report on the victim recovered near Camille's home sent by Florence police nearly a dozen times, but not a single word registered. Because of her. Because the second the words had left his mouth that she was nothing more than his witness, the hollowness he'd lived with since he'd been a ten-year-old spread. He'd been an ass, but that didn't alter the truth. This job took enough of him and enough of his concentration without him having to worry about someone else relying on him to make it through the front door. Someone who might be put in danger because of the nature of his work.

He'd had relationships in the past. A few weeks here, a couple months there. Nothing serious and nothing long-term. He moved around the state enough with his assignments that run-ins were far and few between, and that was the way he liked to keep it. But with Camille... There was nothing casual about her. She'd been engaged, ready to commit herself to one man for the rest of her life. In the end, that man turned out to be a serial killer, but before that, before she'd known how familiar evil could be, she'd been prepared to jump off the cliff of holy matrimony. Prepared to give herself to somebody else, to trust them completely. His heart slammed against his rib cage. Had anyone trusted him that way?

Finn pushed to his feet, tossing his phone onto the mattress. There wasn't any way in hell he was going to be able to read that report with her doing her best to ignore him for the rest of the time they were forced to spend together. The mattress dipped with his added weight as he took a seat, every nerve ending he owned strung tight at the urge to sweep her hair out of her face and make her look at him. "You think we can break our record of using the silent treatment against each other for another hour?"

"Guess there's only one way to find out, isn't there?" She refolded the same shirt she'd been working on a few minutes ago, still refusing to look at him. "And if you only came over here to raid your stash of chocolate, I've got bad news for you. I ate it all when you weren't looking."

"Can't say I didn't deserve that." Finn caught sight of the empty silver foil ripped to shreds beside her. Goose bumps trailed down the backs of his arms as she smoothed the sheets where he'd laid next to her a few hours ago. He'd fallen asleep with her pressed against him from shoulder to toes, as though she'd subconsciously sought him out in the middle of the night, and an illogical part of him wanted to experience the feeling of being needed for something other than hired muscle again. "What I meant earlier was it's my job to keep you alive, Camille. That's my only concern—to make sure you walk away after the trial with your heart beating as strong as when you came into the program. If I'm the smallest bit distracted from that job, it could cost you your life. Or mine. Do you understand?"

"Of course, I understand." She stuffed her folded clothing back into the duffel bag one piece at a time, but her tone and jerking movements suggested they weren't on the same page at all. "You've got a job to do, and everything you've said or done over the past year has been because of this assignment. Not because you led me to believe we're friends, or because you actually give a damn about my mental and emotional well-being. As long as my heart is still beating when this is over, you get to move onto your next detail with a clear conscience." She slid off the bed and got to her feet. "Thank you for clearing up my misconceptions about our relationship and assuming that because I've shown you the slightest bit of appreciation for saving my life that I wanted to get into your pants."

Oh, hell. That wasn't— He hadn't meant it like that. "Camille, I didn't—"

"Don't worry, Marshal. I'll try to make this easier for you from now on." She set fiery aquamarine eyes on him, and the hairs on the back of his neck stood on end. "The next time I'm having difficulty processing the fact a man I used to share a bed with is trying to kill me and a bunch of other women for no discernible reason I can come up with, I'll be sure to keep my mouth shut and deal with it on my own. Like the good witness I'm supposed to be."

She brushed past him toward the kitchen. Lucky for him, there weren't too many places she could run. Not as long as she was under his protection.

"I enlisted as a combat medic because of that night." His gut soured as she slowed in his peripheral vision. When she didn't turn to face him, he studied the uneven rise and fall of her shoulders. "I didn't ever want to be in a position again where I couldn't help someone I cared about. I didn't want to have to stand there and watch them be taken from me, and it might not seem like it, but I care about you, damn it. Probably more than I should. Definitely more than I have with any other witness." He got to his feet. His skin still felt hot where she'd set her hand over his heart before. He couldn't imagine how hard that'd been for her—to reach out to another person, to reach out to him when he'd needed it. Even after everything she'd been through, she'd somehow broken past her instinct to stay in the shadows and walked back out into the light. Now it was his turn. "So if I'm being honest, there's nothing you can do to make this easy for me, Red. Every minute that psychopath is out there hunting you is another shard being driven deeper into my lungs. I know from experience that any one of those minutes could be your last, and I don't want to be the one responsible for that."

Her hands fisted at her sides before she slowly turned around. The black long-sleeve shirt she'd replaced his T-shirt with folded across her midsection as she crossed her arms, the movement accentuating the hues of blue and purple around her throat. Her mouth softened at the corners, but there was still hesitation in the soft outline of her lips. "Finn, I—"

His phone pinged from the end of the bed. Then again… Scooping the damn thing off the comforter, Finn moved to put the device on silent. Then he read the message. Defeat washed through him as reality pierced through the bubble they'd created in this small place. As much as he wanted to live in the fantasy she'd told him of nothing existing outside of these four walls, that wasn't how the world worked. As long as the Carver was out still there, still hunting, Finn wouldn't let down his guard. Couldn't. No matter what happened, he wasn't going to lose anyone else. "Jonah sent over the autopsy report for the woman killed near your house. Jodie Adler."

"Go ahead. I think we've more than made up for the hour we weren't talking to each other." She lowered her arms to her sides, then turned her attention to his personal duffel bag a few feet away. "Jeff—the Carver—was proud of what he'd done to all those women. I could see it in his eyes when he…" She motioned to her neck, then tugged the cuffs of her shirt into her palms and closed her fingers around the edge of fabric. Pulling back her shoulders, Camille smoothed her expression. "Why would he change the order of how he hurt me the second time?"

"In my experience, MOs are unique to a serial killer like Jeff Burnes, the same as fingerprints are unique to human beings. For him and others like him, killing is a compulsive need, and the only way he can get satisfaction from the kill is by following an obsessive routine. Serial killers can evolve over time. They can get smarter, they can hide what they're doing better or they can lose complete control of themselves, but they rarely vary from that core routine. It's the only way they know how to get what they need from their victim. So it doesn't make sense for the Carver to suddenly forget the order he prefers to attack his target." Surprise pulsed through him as he realized why she'd been staring so intently at his overnight bag. The file he'd hidden inside. The Carver's file. His boots reverberated off the tiled floor as he met her in the center of room, then offered her the phone with the crime-scene report open on the screen. "But I don't think you're misremembering what happened, either."

The weight of vulnerability in her gaze stole the air from his lungs. Her breath shuddered as she stared down at the device, but she didn't move to take it from him. "What are you doing?"

"You know this case better than anyone out there, you know him, and you survived." He knew what he was asking. He knew exactly how much trouble he could get in by sharing this information with a civilian, but if he was going to protect his witness against the oncoming threat, he had to know—without a doubt—which direction that threat was coming from. "You're the only one who can tell us if the Carver killed Jodie Adler, Camille."

The bruising along her throat shifted with her swallow. "And if I'm wrong?"

"Then I'll spend the rest of my life on your protection detail, and you'll owe me an entire stash of mattress chocolate." The inside joke cut through the tension faster than he could draw his weapon, and she laughed. An amazing sound. One he never wanted to forget when this was over.

"One file." She took the phone, the brightness of the screen highlighting flawless skin, and maneuvered around him to sit on the edge of the bed. She rolled the hem of her shirt between the index finger and thumb of her free hand, rubbing the fabric back and forth under her thumbnail. She swiped her opposite thumb across the screen, past Florence PD's initial report, before settling on the crime-scene photos. Her eyebrows drew inward a split second before Camille shot to her feet. "Finn, we have to get to that scene. Now."

SHE'D BEEN IMPRISONED in the small town of Florence, Oregon, for a year, cut off from everything she'd known, everyone she'd cared about. But the past had still come back to haunt her.

Shouldering out of Finn's SUV, she battled for mental balance as her unofficial prison cell came into focus. Moisture from the river clung to the exposed skin of her face and neck, the soft sound of ripples lapping from the shoreline. It really was beautiful out here, but while tourists from all over the world flooded into the sleepy coastal city that played home to such beautiful wonders, she'd only felt more isolated. Alone.

The sun clung to the tops of the pines surrounding the property and would vanish well below the tree line in the next thirty minutes. They had to move fast. She slammed the car door behind her, attention sliding to the unpaved trail leading deeper into the woods beyond the property. She pointed to the opening between the trees. "You can get to the scene from that trail there, but I need to get something from the house first."

"You're sure about this?" Finn rounded the hood of the vehicle, armed with a flashlight in one hand and a weapon in his shoulder holster. As much as she'd hated the idea of coming back here, having him with her softened the rough edges of her anxiety. "The crime-scene techs have been over every inch of these woods since the body has been discovered. Several times."

"They didn't know what they were looking for. I do." Camille headed toward the front door of the house, hesitant to walk back into the lonely life of the woman who'd lived here for the past year. But she forced herself to turn the doorknob and push inside. Jodie Adler needed her to be strong, to face the possibility that the Carver had started his sick, twisted cycle of obsession all over again. That just because she'd changed her name didn't mean the killer had forgotten her. Finn's boots echoed loudly through the empty kitchen, hiking her nervous system into overdrive. She moved automatically, step by step, until she reached the hallway. Then slowed.

"Camille?" he asked.

A black-and-white flash of rose petals perfectly placed along the hallway rushed to the front of her mind. She reached for the wall as slices of the adrenaline-fueled minutes that followed threatened to drag her back to that night, but she hit a mountain of muscle instead. Finn. Curling her fingers into his shirt, she shook her head as reality broke through the panic clawing up her throat. "I'm okay. I just… It's all coming back in one giant wave that I can't stop."

Callused fingers wound around her wrist, his thumb pressing against the sensitive skin below her palm. Her pulse pitched against his touch as he tugged her closer. His body heat penetrated through her clothing and straight past muscle and into her bones. "I'm right here. Everything we do here, we do together. You're not alone this time."

She knew that. No matter what happened, he'd protect her because it was his job, but the dark hole of nothingness that had set up residence in her chest since the attack a year ago reminded her his protection only applied to her physical body. Nothing more. Despite his promise that they'd face this threat together, he'd outright told her the emotional connection she'd thrived on since the attack would only be one-sided.

"Thank you." She released her grip on his shirt and stepped completely into the hallway. She was sure the first door on the right—the one just before her bedroom—had been closed by one of the law-enforcement officers after they'd finished processing the scene. Finn's warmth stayed with her as she twisted the knob and swung the door open. She flipped on the light. She faced two rows of seemingly empty picture frames leaning against the walls, but as she edged closer, color bled into focus. Photographs. Some of the very last ones she'd taken. Tentatively reaching out for the first frame, Camille swept dust from the wood. She peeled a smaller frame from against the wall, air building in her chest before she finally had the thought to exhale, and handed him the photo. "This is it."

Surprise or confusion, she wasn't sure which, drew his eyebrows together and deepened the lines across his forehead as he studied the shot. He smoothed the same fingers that'd been grasped around her wrist across the glass. "This looks like—"

"The exact location where Jodie Adler's body was found." She folded her arms across her chest, a meaningless protection against all the pieces of her life showcased in these frames surrounding her. Every photograph in this room represented the woman she'd been before the attack, but the photo clutched in Finn's grip memorialized the one who'd died at the hands of the Carver. "When I relocated to Florence, I couldn't leave this house. I couldn't talk to anyone without getting suspicious of their motivations for wanting to get to know me. I couldn't sleep, and when my body forced me to, all I could see was his face when I closed my eyes."

She intertwined her fingers together and spread her elbows wide. "Within a couple of days, I barely recognized myself in the mirror, and I knew I had to get help. So I started seeing a trauma therapist in town. Dr. Gruner. He didn't know me. He didn't know about the case. But by the time I left his office that first session, he'd convinced me to pick up my camera for the first time since the attack and try to reclaim that part of me Jeff Burnes had taken. To just go somewhere quiet, somewhere I felt safe. I picked that spot and managed to take a single photo before the memories of all those women had a chance to take over."

Finn met her gaze. "It's beautiful."

"That's not why I wanted to show you this picture." Taking the photograph from him, Camille studied the sweeping effect of light across half of the shot, then crouched and slammed the frame onto the hardwood. Glass burst into dozens of jagged pieces at her feet, slicing white lines into the surface of the photo.

"What are you doing?" he asked.

She tipped the framed to get rid of the excess glass. Using her nails, she pried the paper from the frame, turning it over to the back. "This is why I needed you to see it."

She pointed to the date stamped on the back of the photo in the top right corner. Almost one year before the exact date Jodie Adler's body had been found in the location this photograph was taken. "I took this photo a couple weeks after I was relocated to Oregon, and whoever killed Jodie Adler knew that. They knew where I was relocated. They knew how I was attacked and where to place her body to get my attention."

"How is that possible?" Glass skidded across the floor between them as he stepped into her and took the photo from her hand.

"I don't know, but it's too much of a coincidence, don't you think? Almost a year after I take this shot another victim is found in that location killed using the Carver's MO." A shiver chased down her spine. "Whoever killed her might have escaped, but Jeff Burnes was still behind bars when I went out there that day, and I've never had this photograph published. This is the only copy. There's no way he could've known I was in that clearing that day or gotten his hands on this photo."

Not without help.

"You said your therapist urged you to pick up your camera. Dr. Gruner." Finn's voice dipped into dangerous territory as he locked sea-colored eyes on her. "Did you tell him where you'd taken the shot or show him the digital file in one of your follow-up sessions?"

"I…" She felt the blood drain from her face in a rush. Nausea rolled through her stomach and weakened the backs of her knees. No. No, no, no, no. Shaking her head, she mentally tallied all of the details she'd revealed in those therapy sessions from her attack. She recounted the interest in his expression when he asked her to walk him through it again.

This was her fault. Jodie Adler was dead because of her. Just like all those other victims she could've saved if she'd seen Jeff Burnes for the killer he was. Darkness closed in around the edges of her vision, and it wasn't until pain blossomed in her chest that Camille realized she'd been holding her breath. "I dropped my camera after I took the photo. I couldn't get those images of all of Jeff's victims out of my head, and I ended up breaking the LCD panel. I had to print the photo out to show him I was serious about doing the work it'd take to get my life back."

Only now, she realized, it was possible he'd been

using her as a conduit to the man in her nightmares. Why? Her hand grazed the lacerations Finn had dressed, and she froze. The change in MO. The man who'd attacked her had finished carving the letters into her chest before strangling her. He'd broken the Carver's routine. Because it hadn't been her former fiancé that night. It'd been Dr. Gruner.

"I need to call this in to my team." Finn bolted for the door, his phone already in his hand as he retraced their steps to the front of the house. He spoke into the phone without looking back at her, and suddenly the gouges carved into her chest burned. "It's Reed. Get Remi on the line. She's going to want to hear this."

The obsession with her case, the repeated attempts to get her to tell him what'd happened that Valentine's Day over and over. Dr. Henry Gruner hadn't been trying to help her recover from the trauma of surviving a serial killer's attack at all. He'd been trying to get the details right. So he could hunt his own victims.

Bile worked up her throat. Air. She needed air. Camille ran for the sliding glass door off the kitchen. Wrenching the door to her left, she bolted from the house and ran across the property, her legs growing heavy as she neared the tree line. A cold breeze swept off the surface of the river and pushed her hair behind her. Goose pimples prickled the skin around her neck and arms as she weighted both hands onto her knees. She couldn't breathe, couldn't think. Tears streaked down her face and fell into the lush soil under her feet. Her hands shook as she pressed a hand over her mouth and screamed as hard as she could into her palms. Sobs wracked through her, bringing her to her knees.

A twig snapped under pressure from the tree line just before the outline of a masked man solidified. "Hello, Camille. I've been looking for you."

Chapter Seven

The scream made his neck muscles jump. Finn ripped the phone from his ear and twisted back toward the house. He withdrew his weapon and yelled into the phone. "I need every available unit and deputy at Camille Goodman's house. Now!"

He thrust the phone into his coat pocket, not even sure if he'd ended the call with his chief deputy, Remington Barton. It didn't matter. He recognized the source of that scream.

Camille.

Shadows engulfed him on either side as he ran through the front door. Silence echoed off the plain walls, hiking his blood pressure higher. He'd left her in the second bedroom, but the sheer white curtains hanging above the sliding glass door lifted off the hardwood floor with a burst of wind. The door had been left wide open. But had she gone outside or had someone come in? "Camille?"

No answer.

His heart pounded hard behind his ears as he moved through the kitchen and into the small living room, just as he'd done last night after her message for help. Finn rounded into the hallway. Empty. The door to the guest bedroom had been left wide open, but a quick scan revealed she wasn't inside. Damn it. He checked the master bedroom and the single bathroom. No sign of her. "Where the hell are you, Red?"

Retracing his steps, he approached the sliding glass door. It was too quiet. Camille wouldn't have run off on her own, wouldn't intentionally hide from him or leave. Not with a killer placing her in his sights. Which meant the SOB who'd attacked her ago had come to finish the job.

He swept one curtain panel out of the way, meeting nothing but the long expanse of property and darkness over the splintered back deck. The photo connecting Camille to Jodie Adler's death scene demanded attention from inside his jacket pocket as old wood protested under his weight. There was no way Jeff Burnes would've known about the photograph Camille had taken or that specific location near her property, which meant whoever'd killed Jodie Adler had to have intimate knowledge of her movements, of that photograph and the specific details of the Carver's kills that'd never been released to the public.

Her therapist. Dr. Henry Gruner.

He'd been watching her. Stalking her. Using their sessions against her so he could bide his time until the perfect moment and he had the chance to strike. Only that didn't explain why the Carver had escaped federal custody, how he played into this mind game or where he was now. Finn honed in on the sway of the trees outlining a nearly invisible trailhead at the edge of the property. "I'll be damned."

Memories of the night of the attack played across his mind. The feeling of being watched as he'd rushed Camille out of the house, the prickling of his instincts when he'd tried to force his senses to adjust through the haze of adrenaline. Studying the angle between that trailhead and the sliding glass doors, Finn was fairly certain at that vantage point, anyone could walk out of those woods and get close enough to the house without catching Camille's attention from inside.

That was where the killer had vanished that night.

That was where he'd left his latest victim to be found.

That was where the bastard had taken Camille.

Digging for his flashlight in his back pocket, he pressed the power button and jogged for the trailhead. Two minutes—maybe three—since her scream had turned his blood cold. The bastard couldn't have gotten far. A burst of wind threatened to knock him off course before he hit the tree line. Rain had started, drops plastering to his face, but that wouldn't slow him down. He followed the unpaved trail deeper into the woods, damp soil clinging to his boots. The wind picked up, the rain fell harder. Didn't matter. It was his job to protect his witness, and that was exactly what he was going to do. No matter the cost.

"Finn!" Terror echoed in her voice, pushing him harder.

The trail split in two directions ahead, and Finn slowed. His breath sawed in and out of his lungs as he jerked the flashlight beam over the ground. Where was she? The rain, combined with the entire team of forensic investigators who'd processed Jodie Adler's crime scene, had already compromised any tracks the killer might've left behind. He couldn't tell the difference in treads or when each divot in the dirt had been made. His heart nearly beat straight out of his chest as the chance of finding her alive dwindled with every moment he second-guessed himself. "Camille!"

Drops of water slid into his vision, the hard rain suctioning his clothing to his skin. He couldn't wait. Couldn't stop. Pumping his legs as hard as he could, Finn followed the trail on the left, gun in hand. There was no sign of her. No more calls for help. Twigs scratched at the exposed skin on his face and neck as the natural path carved through the trees narrowed, then disappeared altogether before it ended at a stretch of dark shoreline of Siuslaw River. Glimmers of moonlight distorted across the jagged surface of the river as rain pelted into the shallows, and the breath rushed out of him as realization hit. "No. Damn it, no."

He'd chosen the wrong trail.

He'd lost her.

Strengthening his grip on his weapon, Finn turned back.

A fist slammed into his face. Lightning raced across his vision, his eyes watering as he smashed against the nearest tree. The gun fell from his hand into the bushes along the narrow trail, but before he could dive for the weapon, another hit rocked his head back into the tree. Dizziness rolled through him, but Finn managed to stay on his feet. "Not cool."

The outline of his attacker blocked the trail leading back the way he'd come.

Every cell in his body focused entirely on the one thing keeping him from getting to his witness. The masked SOB who'd taken her, who'd tried to kill her. Who'd killed an innocent woman to draw Camille into his sick game. But Finn wasn't going to lose her. Not like this. Straightening, he faced off with the man he recognized as the masked attacker he'd fought the night of Camille's attack. "Where is she, you son of a bitch?"

The suspect reached toward his lower back, and pulled a long, gleaming blade. The sound of rain on steel reached his ears a mere moment before his attacker sliced the knife down across Finn's chest. Stinging pain burned across his skin as his attacker threw another punch. Finn dodged the attempt and slammed his fist into the suspect's jaw. Seeing an opening, he shoved the bastard off balance, but it wasn't enough. Camille's abductor spun, then followed up with another ear-ringing hit to Finn's temple.

In an instant, bark cut into his back and head as his attacker hauled him against the tree. An explosion of agony ripped through him as Finn took another hard left to the face. He was pinned. His opponent was stronger, faster, more skilled, but he wasn't going to leave Camille in the hands of a killer. Kicking out, he connected his heel into his opponent's knee and brought him down. He threw everything he had into knocking out his attacker with one final strike, but the world suddenly tilted on its axis as his legs were swept out from under him. Pain arced down his spine and across his neck as he crashed down on an exposed tree root. His head snapped back.

Camille. He had to get to Camille.

The suspect, who was lying beside him, hadn't

said a word, but Finn didn't have to hear the bastard's voice to know who was behind the mask.

"I know you've been watching her, Dr. Gruner, and I know why." Rolling onto his side, he clocked the son of a bitch as the man tried to get to his feet to buy himself a few more seconds. Finn pushed upright, but a solid kick to his rib cage knocked the air from his lungs. His arms and knees collapsed right out from under him, and he landed hard on his front. His lungs groaned for the slightest hint of air.

Stinging pain exploded across his skull as Dr. Gruner grabbed a fistful of his hair and dragged him off the trail. Finn swung out for contact but missed. Ice sparked through his nerve endings as his attacker tossed him down a short decline to the river's shore. Broken twigs, dead foliage and mud clung to his clothing as he slid into the first foot of river water. His ribs protested with sharp inhales as the hiss of knee-high grass reached through the consistent pattering of rain across the river's surface. Pressure wedged between his shoulder blades with the help of the killer's boot, and Finn screamed out.

His head dipped beneath the water's surface.

Pressing his palms into the crumbling soil beneath him, he couldn't get solid purchase to hoist himself out. Not with the added weight on his back and possible broken ribs. Bubbles escaped his mouth and tickled along his face as he tried to wrench free of

Dr. Gruner's hold. His lungs burned as algae and cold water battled for entry into his mouth and nose. No. This wasn't how it was going to end. He wasn't going to leave Camille to fight this monster on her own.

She'd spent the past year in hiding, scared, alone, and damn it, she deserved better. She deserved someone to stand up for her, to fight for her. Make her feel safe and in control of her life for once.

Finn tried to calm his body's automatic panic enough to focus on finding something—anything—he could use as a weapon. He sifted through the loose dirt and debris that'd collected beneath the surface, intentionally slowing his movements. The more he struggled, the faster he'd burn through his oxygen supply. His finger grazed a long, flat rock a few inches below the silt, and he grabbed it with everything he had left before jerking his back into the killer's boots. Once. Twice.

Then he waited.

The weight of Dr. Gruner's boot disappeared from between his shoulder blades, but before the bastard could get his balance, Finn rocketed to his feet and swept the rock's edge across the killer's neck.

The thin shale dissolved on impact in his hand.

"Well, that didn't go as planned." In his next breath, gut-wrenching agony ripped through his middle. His heels sank low in the mud as he stumbled back. Finn studied the rivulets of water forming long lines from the blade's handle straight into the left side of his body.

Then collapsed back into the river.

HER STOMACH ROLLED with the sway of the floor underneath her.

Camille tasted the bile sticking to the sides of her mouth and pressed her forehead into the cold, hard wood. Her mouth had dried from screaming and her throat was raw as it'd been twenty-four hours ago, but her clothing was soaked through. Where…?

The floor rolled again, and she opened her eyes. Dark curtains nearly blended into the blackness through two windows on the other side of the small space. A minimalist set of folding chairs, with a short round table between them, had been arranged against the wall, their feet sliding toward her with slow waves passing beneath her. The single lamp on a desk tucked into the corner highlighted lime-green walls with turquoise accents. A trundle bed took up most of the space at her back. Minimal decoration. No personal effects. No way to tell where her attacker had brought her.

Nausea crested with another wave. She'd been knocked unconscious to stop her from screaming for Finn. So her abductor couldn't have taken her far. She had to still be in Florence. Rotating her head back over her shoulder, she tugged at the ties securing her wrists behind her back and her ankles. The space was too large for a boat, but with the motion of the floor, a houseboat made sense as a possibility.

Something secluded, easily accessible and impossible to escape quickly, depending whether or not he'd taken her to open water.

She couldn't hold back the groan that escaped from her lips. A tremor coursed from the top of her head straight down to her toes as reality set in. She'd been abducted from her property, knocked unconscious and relocated. Did the marshals even know she was missing? Did Finn? The last day of conversations with the deputy assigned to protect her lit up a part of her she'd tried to keep buried over the past year. The part that'd tried to convince her nobody who hadn't survived what she'd survived could understand her, would give up trying and would cut their losses when they realized they'd be better off without her. She'd handed him proof that all of this— the manipulation games, Jodie Adler's death, the Carver's obsessive need for revenge—had all been because of her. It'd been her fault. She was the reason he'd been brought on the case, why he'd become as much of a target as she had. Despite his assignment given to him by the marshals service, she'd put him in the same position his mother had when she'd been shot all those years ago because she wasn't strong enough to face this evil alone. By casting him as her only defense against her past, she'd brought the threat into his life, and Camille hated herself for it.

"Finn?" Her voice failed. No answer. The past raced to meet the present in a violent rush of memory and emotional loneliness. The dull ache at the base of her head intensified as she rolled onto one arm and used the swaying motion of the house to sit upright. Back pressed against the bed, she held her strained breath and pulled her wrists apart as hard as she could. Plastic dug into the thin skin below her palms, right where her pulse had pressed against Finn's thumb when he'd promised they were in this together, but she didn't feel like she was part of a partnership now. This felt like the first time she'd stood in that big house that didn't belong to her all by herself. She'd been ordered to stay in a town she wasn't familiar with, where she didn't know anyone, where she couldn't talk to anyone without lying. No more interrogations by the FBI. No more personal protection detail from the marshals. No one to talk to more than once a month. Once again, her attacker had made her feel utterly empty and alone.

An invisible quake hitched her insides. Dr. Henry Gruner had taken her vulnerabilities, the access she'd given him to her darkest, most painful self and used it against her and an innocent woman. Why? He was supposed to be the one to help her heal, help her move on, but he'd only dragged her back into a nightmare she couldn't escape.

Her fantasy self, the one she'd always looked up to, would be brave. She wouldn't be sitting here wondering why she'd become the obsession of a psychopath or playing the victim. She'd notch her chin higher and think of a way out of these zip ties, then figure out where she was and how hard it would be to get to shore.

Camille closed her eyes, envisioning every thought, every move that imaginary self would make. Her abductor wouldn't leave her alone for long, and she couldn't take the risk of sticking around to confirm who was behind that dark ski mask. She opened her eyes. She had to find something to cut through the zip ties and get back to the house. Had to find Finn.

She didn't care that Finn had shut down any chance of their roles becoming something more than witness and protector. Whether Dr. Gruner was behind that mask or the Carver had come to finish the job he'd started last Valentine's Day didn't matter. They didn't just hurt their victims. They destroyed their lives and the lives of the people they cared about the most, and Finn didn't deserve to suffer because of her. The letters carved into her chest had burned as a constant reminder of what she'd lost, but Finn had somehow soothed the shame and hatred she'd carried since their bloodied inception with a single change in dressing. He'd taken his time with her when she'd jerked out of his reach, made her feel safe and important. More than anyone ever had. Their combined love of the same brand of chocolate and quirky inside jokes had forged a connection she hadn't expected to feel with anyone again. But what she really didn't understand was the bizarre, illogical need to savor the softness and clean, laundered scent of one of his superhero T-shirts one more time. Maybe if she'd kept the one he'd loaned her, uncertainty and fear wouldn't have such a tight hold on her now.

A prickle of unease crawled up the back of her neck as she propped her bound hands on the floor behind her and shifted to the right. There was a small desk on the other side of the bed. Maybe something inside would be sharp enough to cut through the plastic around her wrists and ankles.

Another wave rolled beneath the houseboat, and Camille pitched onto her side with a thud. Soft petals brushed against her face. Red rose petals. Like the ones that'd fallen to the floor in her Chicago apartment after Jeff Burnes had attacked her from across the table on the evening of Valentine's Day. Five seconds passed. Ten. Her breath shuddered out of her in short bursts.

Then footsteps registered from somewhere outside.

Panic gut-punched her into action. Wrenching herself off the floor, she ignored the agony of hard wood biting into her knees when the zip ties refused to stretch and scooted toward the desk in the corner. She hauled herself into a seated position, her head level with the first drawer in a stack of three, but she had no way of opening it without her hands free.

A shadow crossed in front of the main windows, highlighted by veins of moonlight cutting through a bank of cloudy sky. She stilled. Curtains covered the panes, similar to the panels she'd hung along the sliding glass door in her house. Were they thick enough to keep her attacker from seeing her inside? Her heart hammered as the shadow passed to the other side of the structure, but she couldn't relax yet. Not until she was safely on shore.

Camille pressed her back into the narrow space between the desk's edge and the side of the bed and shifted her weight onto her heels. Caked mud on the bottom of her shoes threatened to make her lose traction, and she locked her back teeth in an effort to stay quiet. Muscle by muscle, she hiked her legs and tailbone off the floor until she stood. Tingling numbness spiked through her hands, but she still had enough feeling left to curve one hand around the small wooden knob of the drawer. Carefully, she tugged on the drawer, mindfulness of her abductor's proximity screaming warning in her head. One wrong move. That was all it would take, and the Carver would get exactly what he'd wanted when he'd attacked her in their shared apartment back in Chicago. Only it was possible Jeff Burnes wouldn't be the one to claim her in the end. "Come on."

Old hardware protested as she slid the drawer outward, and every nerve in her body caught fire at the overly loud sound.

The door into the house burst open, slamming back into the wall behind it. Rain pounded onto the shoulders of the man who'd taken her as he filled the frame, and panic took control of her. "I was beginning to think I'd hit you too hard. Now the fun can really begin, and not even your US marshal will be able to save you this time."

His arm angled down toward his waist, and he withdrew a long, thin blade.

"What do you want from me?" Thrusting her hands into the drawer, Camille blindly searched for a weapon that could cut through the zip ties, but her fingers only met dried, unfinished wood. Fear clawed behind her sternum, her gut tight. She curled her fingers into fists to tighten the plastic as much as possible. There was only one way out of this nightmare.

Through the man who'd brought her here in the first place.

Her shoulder bumped into a framed photo positioned on the wall behind her. The frame hit the hardwood floor at her feet corner first, glass shattering everywhere. This was it. This was how she'd escape. But could she move fast enough before her abductor reached her?

"Haven't you figured it out yet, Camille?" His boots reverberated on the hardwood flooring and up her legs. The way he walked, the way he talked... Nothing about him was familiar. She didn't know this man. Not as Jeff Burnes. Not as Dr. Henry Gruner. "I want everything."

Camille dropped down and scooped a long, jagged piece of glass from the floor. In one swipe, she cut through the zip ties around her ankles. The hulking mountain of muscle charged toward her, and a dark, cold fear unfurled in her chest. She wasn't going to make it. She tightened her grip around the glass as she managed to cut through the plastic, brought her hands around to her front and braced for the impact.

The shard pierced through clothing and deep into flesh, forcing her attacker to pull up short. Her hand shook as she peeled her fingers from around the piece of glass. Blood bloomed inside her palm, and she released the breath she hadn't realized she'd been holding. She'd stabbed him.

He stumbled back a step, but faster than she thought possible, the man behind the mask ripped the makeshift weapon from his gut and stabbed it into her shoulder. Agonizing pain tore a scream from her throat as blackness webbed around her vision, and she fell back against the wall. "I've always liked a fighter."

Chapter Eight

Hell, he felt like he was floating through endless space with nothing to anchor him.

A groan rumbled through his chest as Finn rolled onto his side, aggravating the wound in his gut. Half of his body had been submerged under water, but he'd managed to pull himself to shore. Rain mixed with blood, dripping from his T-shirt and falling into the marshlike shoreline of the river. His veins strained through his forearms as he pushed onto all fours. Rain lashed at his exposed skin and created a million pits and bubbles on the surface of the water. Cold crawled up the back of his neck.

There was no way to stop the bleeding out here. Not without something to staunch the flow. Under normal circumstances he'd have access to clean water and medical supplies, but the past hour had been anything but normal. He'd seen plenty of cases of penetrating abdominal trauma during his two tours in the Middle East. Mostly from shrapnel, rarely from hand-to-hand combat, but the same principles applied. Apply pressure to stop the bleeding, clean the area and patch. Although, out here, he might have to skip a couple steps. With Camille still missing, possibly in the hands of a killer, he didn't have much of a choice. It was either risk infection or leave her to fight for herself.

His mind was already made up.

His calf muscles strained as he struggled for balance and got to his feet. The incline he'd rolled down during the fight was slick with rainwater and mud, but he didn't see any other way around it. He'd taken the wrong trail in his desperation to follow her screams, had given her abductor the opportunity to get the drop on him, and now his witness was in danger. Because he'd made a mistake.

Finn pressed one hand into his gut and locked his back teeth to bite back the scream of pain as he forced one foot in front of the other. Step by agonizing step, he hauled himself up the slick incline, the muscles down the backs of his legs on fire. He couldn't stop. No matter how much it hurt. He didn't care if his accelerated heart rate pumped blood out through the wound faster. He wasn't giving up on Camille.

He dug his free hand into the mud and clawed the last few feet until the ground under him leveled, then fell onto his back. Lungs fighting for air, he blinked against a bright streak of lightning flashing over him. Trees creaked with steady gusts of wind and rain, as though this entire section of woods understood the war tearing him apart from the inside.

He couldn't lose her. He'd spent his entire life training and preparing for this job, had handled over a dozen witness-protection details, but in less than two mind-twisting days this assignment had already ripped the world right out from under him. But if he was being completely honest with himself, it wasn't the case.

Camille had defied the assigned role he'd given her and broken through his determination to keep their interactions professional without even trying. Despite the odds stacked against her, he couldn't help but marvel at the fact that each time she'd been knocked down, she'd gotten right back up, ready for the next threat. She'd survived. He wasn't sure how. How, even with being betrayed by someone she trusted so intimately—once by Jeff Burnes and then by her therapist, Dr. Gruner—she hadn't let it break her. She'd lost parts of herself, that much he'd seen for himself, but the woman was still standing. Still fighting.

And so would he.

"Okay." Finn raised the back of his head off the ground and lifted his shirt to get a clear view of the wound. Blood seeped down in long riverlike threads across his abdomen with the help of the unforgiving storm. Setting his head back, he gripped the bottom of his shirt between both hands and ripped the hem from the main body. All he needed was a long strip of fabric and something to pad the wound. He used one foot to toe off his boot, then crunched down to slip his sock from his foot. It was rudimentary, but the sock and makeshift tourniquet would keep the wound dry and infection-free until he could get to a hospital.

Images of that night a man had followed his mother home and shot her right in front of him demanded priority as he folded the sock in half and set it against the stab wound. He'd been alone then, too. Only now he had someone to fight for. Finn threaded the strip of fabric underneath him and wound the ends together. He took a deep breath, preparing for the oncoming pain, then tightened the knot against the dressing as fast and as hard as he could.

White streaks spread across his vision before he collapsed back into the mud. Oxygen whooshed from his lungs, but he couldn't waste any more time. Rolling onto his side, he set his fist in front of his face and pushed upright with everything he had left. Recognition flared as he studied the narrowing wall of trees to his left. The dead end. If he followed the trail back to where he'd taken the wrong turn, he'd be one step closer to finding his witness.

He closed in on the tree his attacker had pinned him against when he'd lost his weapon, sweeping brush and leaves out of the way until he found his firearm. The steel heavy in his grip, Finn released the magazine out of the gun with bloodied knuckles, counted the rounds and cleared the chamber. He stumbled along the path until he hit the fork in the trail. "I'm coming for you, Red. Just hang on a little bit longer. Hang on for me."

There was only one thing that mattered: getting her out of here alive. Not the boundaries he'd set between them. Not his past or his fear of losing the people he cared about. Her. She was all that mattered, and he wasn't going to stop until he found her. A muscle spasmed in his side, and he fell against the nearest tree. The wind picked up, howling through the branches and fluttering leaves. An ache washed through him, something visceral and gut-wrenching.

Grief took him by surprise like that sometimes. It tended to blindside him when he least expected it, then took his mind on a joyride through a past he'd rather forget. Lodging in his chest, the darkness took control faster than he expected until he couldn't move, couldn't think. He hadn't been able to help his mother all those years ago. He'd only been a kid. He knew that, but it didn't make the guilt festering under his skin any less real. And if something happened to Camille, he'd never forgive himself.

He hadn't been able to help Deputy US Marshal Karen Reed, but he'd sure as hell protect his witness the same as his mother would have. With his life. Finn dug his fingernails into the tree's bark. The only way he'd be able to pull himself back into the moment, to stay present, was by forcing his brain to think analytically instead of emotionally. Countless hours of trauma therapy as a kid had taught him that. If his grandparents hadn't demanded he go, he wouldn't have been able to make it through two tours for the army or apply to the marshals service. He hadn't appreciated the help at the time, but he'd confronted the fact he hadn't been the only one to lose his mom that day. His grandparents had lost their daughter, and he owed them enough to try. One breath. Two. Three. He closed his eyes, narrowing his senses into the rise and fall of his chest, the sound of the rain pattering against the leaves surrounding him, the feel of his heart pounding against his rib cage. "Detach, detach, detach."

He could do this. He had to do this. For Camille.

He took a full, deep breath, and the pressure valve behind his sternum released. Opening his eyes, a new sense of awareness and determination replaced the ache that'd ballooned painfully in his chest. He took a strong step forward, calculating where to put his foot next. Then he froze.

Thin white branches jutted out from the underbrush beside his boot, so light in contrast to the surrounding trees and limbs around him. But the longer

Finn studied the curves and smooth texture, the more he realized he wasn't looking at pieces of wood.

They were skeletal remains.

He leaned back to avoid stepping on the bone nearest his boot and swept the bushes covering the remains out of the way. Mud clung to the edges of the skull, the head cocked slightly to one side with a full mouth of teeth seemingly smiling up at him. He wasn't a combat medic anymore, but his training gave him enough of an insight to notice the victim hadn't suffered any head trauma. Only the hyoid bone, the horse-shaped bone situated in the anterior midline of the neck between the chin and the thyroid cartilage, seemed to be broken.

Which could possibly mean whoever this was had been strangled.

Dread pooled at the base of his spine. Two bodies discovered within the past couple days, both strangled and left in these woods near Camille's house. Finn didn't believe in coincidence, but he didn't have time to do a more thorough study, either. His witness needed him. Now.

He pulled out his phone, then swiped water and mud from the screen. The broken glass caught on his thumb. Blood spread to the surface, but he wiped it on his shirt as the screen lit up. Still working. He tapped Jonah Watson's name in his contact list and brought the phone to his ear, not waiting for a greet-

ing when the line connected. "I found human remains out here about a quarter mile from Camille
Goodman's house, maybe as old as a year, possibly
strangled. I'm sending you my location, but I won't
be here by the time you're on the scene. I've got at
least one hostile, armed, and my witness is missing.
I can't stay here with the body. I have to find her."

"We're pulling up to the house now." Jonah's voice
carried over the static breaking through the line. "All
you need to worry about is securing your witness.
We'll take care of everything else."

"Copy that." Finn scanned the trees as he sent
his team his current location. There were a dozen
sites the killer could've taken Camille, but he'd need
somewhere close, somewhere private to finish the
work he'd started. Somewhere he wouldn't be found
or possibly disturbed by tourists who visited this
area throughout the year. "One more thing. I need
you to tell me if Dr. Henry Gruner has any property
in Florence or around Siuslaw River."

"Henry Gruner owns a houseboat not far from
the coordinates you just me," the former FBI bomb
technician said. "Florence PD passed along the information when he turned up as a connection between
your witness and the victim we recovered from the
woods. Dr. Gruner was both Camille Goodman's
and Jodie Adler's psychologist."

Finn limped along the trail, heading straight for the darkness. "Send me the coordinates. Now."

"YOU CERTAINLY ARE a beautiful work of art." The mask over her abductor's face shifted with each word, the strong bite of sweat and weak cologne threatening to gag her more than the fabric secured between her lips. He set the cold steel of the blade against the sensitive skin of her cheek and trailed downward, but there was no escaping this time. He'd made sure of that when he'd plunged the shard of glass into her shoulder and forced her into one of the wooden chairs near the window. New zip ties pinned her wrists against splintered wood as he dragged the tip of the knife downward.

A burning trail of sensation carved over her jaw, under her chin, along the muscles in her throat. Until he reached the collar of her shirt. In one masterful swipe of the blade, he exposed the rain-soaked gauze Finn had taped over the word etched into her skin, and it took everything she had left not to flinch away. To withhold the fear he wanted to see from her. "I can see now why he was so set on claiming you as his own—marking you as off-limits to the rest of us— but I'm a believer in making my own fate. Not waiting for permission. After I show him exactly what I'm capable of when I'm finished with you, he'll have no choice but to see I'm stronger than he'll ever be."

"He?" The word drowned behind the damp fabric he'd tied at the base of her skull. Camille swallowed to keep the shudder out of her voice but only managed to bring her attacker's focus back to her throat. She didn't understand. The man standing in front of her wasn't the killer she was familiar with, wasn't Dr. Gruner. At least not based on his voice alone. Everything she and Finn had uncovered connecting to this case pointed to her therapist as their main suspect. Jodie Adler's body being found in the exact location as the photo he'd urged her to take, the information the killer had known about Camille and the attack from that night.

There was only one problem. She didn't know this man.

Curling her fingers around the ends of the chair's arms, she wrenched her head back to keep from passing out. She'd lost a lot of blood when he'd stabbed her with the piece of glass, but she wasn't the only one. Wet stains spread across her kidnapper's dark clothing, and it was only a matter of time before he'd have to do something about it. She just had to buy enough time for Finn to find her. Had to keep him talking.

"The Carver, silly." The upbeat tone in her attacker's voice pooled a fresh dose of dread at the base of her spine. How could a man who satisfied his sick cravings by torturing innocent women sound so...happy about it? The knife gleamed in a sliver of moonlight as he bent down and evened his gaze with hers. Black cutouts in the mask framed generic brown eyes with a hint of blond eyebrows at the corners. Six foot, maybe six-one, and she'd put his weight at around two hundred and twenty pounds. It was a wall of solid muscle she'd become familiar with when he'd ripped her away from her property.

He was right before. He was stronger, faster, better at this than Jeff Burnes, but where she'd hesitated in sinking that blade into her former fiancé, there was nothing that would stop her from protecting herself against this man before he killed her. He straightened. "If it hadn't been for that marshal glued to your side, I would've been able to prove my superiority sooner. Thankfully, he won't be a problem anymore."

What did that mean? She felt the blood drain from her face then tugged at the zip ties as hard as she could. Her shoulder screamed for relief. The plastic wouldn't budge. Her words died behind the gag. "What ?"

"It's kind of ironic." The man with the knife pressed his hand against his wound and rubbed fresh blood between his fingers. "I think this is the same exact spot I stabbed him before I left him to die."

"No." That wasn't possible. She shook her head, fighting to keep the gruesome images at bay, but as a photographer, all her thoughts and inspirations were made possible by visualizing everything in her head. Finn wasn't dead. Her attacker wanted to see her fear, wanted her to scream, sob, deny any of this was happening. That was how sociopaths worked. They couldn't feel emotion themselves. They had to study it from the people around them, from their victims, when hands-off experiments didn't work, and she wasn't going to let him see her break. She'd been manipulated before, and in the end, sharing the same bed with a killer had given her the mental strength to see through the lie. "Don't…believe…you."

Because if Finn was dead, she'd have no one left. No one to appreciate her terrible inside jokes, no one who made her feel safe, no one to connect with. No one to appreciate her as the woman she was now. Not the woman she'd been. She'd been left in the middle of nowhere after the most traumatic event of her life, and he'd been the only one who'd shown her there was a way out.

"That's okay. I don't need you to believe me." Her abductor twirled the tip of his blade into his index finger. Back and forth, back and forth. He stepped into her, his leg brushing the inside of her knee, then pried the gag from her mouth. "What I need is for you to tell me everything you know about Jeff Burnes. I've studied under him a long time since he found me trying to replicate his MO back in Chicago two years ago, but if I'm going to show him how far I've come, that I'm better at this than he is, I need to know where to deliver your body. You're the only one who can help me with that, Camille."

That was what this was about?

"You have no idea who you're trying to prove yourself to." She looked straight into those cold brown eyes for something to focus on other than the pain in her shoulder. "I don't know where he is since he escaped prison. I'm the last person who would know, but I'll tell you one thing—it will be the best day for humanity when you two die trying to kill each other."

A low, terrifying laugh punctured through the hard beat of her pulse, right before pain streaked across her temple and echoed off the inside of her ears. He pulled his gloved fist back for another strike, but the houseboat blurred as the momentum from his punch pushed her and the chair over until she hit the floor. Without her hands to brace for the fall, her head bounced off the hardwood. His footsteps vibrated through the floor and down her back as he moved away from her toward the desk to her left. "You really don't know, do you, Camille?"

A sob escaped her control. Forgetting her wrists were bound by zip ties secured to the chair, she tried to bring her hand to her head. The left chair arm shifted. Raising her gaze to the masked attacker to see if he'd noticed, she shut down the urge to scream and pulled the entire chair arm free from the rest of the frame. Then did the same with the right side. Victory bulldozed the knot of internal fear into submission, but she couldn't celebrate yet. She had to get out of here, had to find Finn.

"I'm the one who broke into your house. I'm the one who finished the work the Carver wasn't strong enough to do." His voice made the hairs on the back of her neck rise as memories of fear—of the pain—infiltrated the thin barrier she'd constructed to forget. The change in the Carver's MO. It wasn't because Jeff Burnes had been trying to throw the police off his trail. It'd been an entirely different killer wielding the knife that'd cut into her. "But I didn't kill that woman by your house. He's been watching you, Camille. Waiting for the perfect opportunity to finish what he started. It was only a matter of time before he made himself known." The man in the mask raised a syringe and tapped the casing to bring the bubbles in the clear liquid to the needle head. "But now it's my turn."

Slipping from the debris as quietly as she could, she discarded the zip ties but held on to one chair arm with as tight a grip as a drowning victim might hold on to a life preserver. One step. Two. "You'll have to get in line."

Her nerves spiked as he turned to face her, and Camille swung the piece of wood as hard as she could across his face. His pain-filled groan filled the small space as he went down, but she didn't wait to find out how much damage she'd caused. Pumping her legs as hard as she could, she ripped the front door nearly off the frame and dashed into the night. With a fleeting glimpse behind her, she ran out into the rain, then pitched forward as something caught her ankles. She slammed onto an old dock, the air knocked from her lungs. A wave of dizziness pitched her sideways as she struggled to get to her feet.

A trip wire.

He'd set a trip wire in case she tried to escape.

Throwing her hands out for balance, she stepped forward, but gut-wrenching pain flared across her scalp as her attacker wrenched her back by her hair. Camille twisted as hard as she could and rocketed her fist into his face. He stumbled back with her still in his grip, but with a final blow to her jaw, she hit the dock.

"I think we're going to have a lot of fun together, Camille," he said.

Pain pelted her face and eyes, the looming dark figure above going in and out of focus. He hauled one of her legs up by her ankle and pulled her back toward the houseboat. Her arms dragged out and up near her head. No. No. She couldn't go back. Camille fought to grab on to something—anything—to keep him from taking her back inside.

Just as three gunshots exploded above.

Chapter Nine

His suspect dropped to the dock.

Finn lowered the gun, but even without the threat of the killer standing over her, Camille wasn't moving.

Blood drained from his head, and the sound of rain hitting the surface of the river turned into nothing more than a buzz in his ears. Then he was running. Knee-high grass whipped at his legs as he closed in on her prone outline. Panic boiled up inside him in a horrible, hot, toxic cocktail and cut off his ability to take a full breath. Old wood swayed under his feet as he hit the dock. "Camille!"

He kicked what looked like a syringe full of some kind of clear drug out of her attacker's hand and tested the SOB's pulse at the base of his neck. Dead. "Stay down this time, you bastard."

Finn turned his attention on Camille. He fell to his knees beside her, threading his hand beneath her soaked hair. Blood spread from a wound in her shoulder, the same side she'd been branded by her attacker, and his gut clenched. A stab wound? He holstered his weapon to keep himself from adding another three rounds into the body of the man who'd nearly taken his witness from him. "Camille?"

The aquamarine eyes that he hadn't gone a single moment without visualizing during his search shot open a split second before her fist connected with his nose. Lightning struck behind his eyes. Her back arched off the dock as she battled tooth and nail to get free, her screams penetrating the wall of buzzing in his head and stabbing straight into his heart. "No! No!"

"Camille! Camille, it's me. It's Finn. I'm not here to hurt you." Tense muscles down her back fought against his touch, but he wasn't going to add to her pain by trying to control her. She was alive. That was all that mattered, and Finn could only wrap his arms around her so she didn't aggravate whatever wound had punctured her shoulder. "I've got you. You're safe with me, Red."

"Finn." The fight drained out of her in an instant, replaced by teeth-shattering tremors. Curling in on herself, she leaned into him as sobs wracked through her. She held one hand closed over her mouth, as though she intended to stop the cries from rushing past her lips, and fisted his shirt with the other.

"It's okay." He pulled her into him, pressing her

head against his chest, and rocked her back and forth. Ducking his mouth to her ear, Finn kept his voice low as he cradled her as close as he could possibly get. Eyeing the body a few feet from them, he shifted his hold on her so she wouldn't have to see her abductor or the houseboat he'd obviously held her in these past couple of hours. "You're okay. It's going to be okay."

She deserved better. Better protection than he'd been able to give, better understanding of what she'd been through. Better than him. He should've stayed with her and not let her out of his sight. Now the woman who'd shattered through the professional barriers he'd built between them would have to live with his mistake. He'd tried to keep his distance, tried to hide behind his fear in an effort to protect himself, but in the end, he'd left his witness to fight this battle alone. Emotionally. Physically. What kind of marshal did that make him? What kind of man? "I'm not going anywhere, okay? I'm going to be right here with you. I promise. No one is going to take you from me again."

Looking back, he realized all she'd been trying to do is connect with someone—anyone—who might want to understand what it'd been like to survive the most distressing experience of her life, and he'd pushed her away. Cut himself off from having to feel more than he should for the woman in his arms. He'd put his own selfish needs ahead of hers, and a killer had nearly claimed her all over again. He couldn't imagine the pain and loneliness she'd had to live with this past year, but as long as she was assigned to his protection detail, he'd make damn sure she never had to feel that emptiness again. "I'm going to get you out of here, okay? I need you to hang on to me and don't let go."

Rain pounded against his face as he slid an arm under the backs of her knees. Soreness tore through his side with her added weight, but that wouldn't stop him from walking her out of this damn forest alive and getting her the help she needed. He lifted her off the dock and headed for the trail that curved back down toward her house.

Each step gained toward the trailhead taught him a new meaning for the word *agony* as he struggled to keep her off her feet, but with her arms tight around his neck, he counted every second she let him hold her worth the lesson. Twenty-four hours ago, she hadn't let him come near her other than to patch the wounds on her chest. Now it seemed the mere thought of releasing him brought more anxiety than before, and he couldn't help but let that fact wash over him.

She was just supposed to be another witness-protection assignment, but Finn had never felt so useless and so capable at the same time as he had with her. The past day had been an internal war tearing

him apart from the inside. On one side was his determination to keep social attachments at a minimum,
something left over from the same grief that'd para-
lyzed him during his search for his witness. And on
the other side was Camille.

Creative, reserved, sensitive Camille. The woman
he hadn't seen coming before she knocked him on
his ass, but she was more than the victim she'd been
labeled as by all the officers assigned to her case.

He'd never frozen while on assignment, least of
all during a protection detail. Not like that. He could
only think of one reason why this investigation might
bring up those desperate, isolated memories of losing his mother that he'd spent the last twenty-five
years burying at the back of his mind. Because this
wasn't just an assignment anymore, and she wasn't
just a witness.

Rivulets of water trailed down her neck and across
her cheeks. It would've been easy for him to bleed out
in those weeds after he'd been stabbed, but it'd been
her example—her fight—that'd given him the strength
to pull himself back from the edge. He might've been
tasked to stand between her past and death, but she
was the only one strong enough to willingly stand
between him and the lingering fear he carried of getting close to the people around him, and damn, he respected the hell out of that. Respected her. He'd spent
most of his life keeping people at a distance, but she'd

shown him how vital those connections really were, and he'd taken them for granted.

Shouts echoed through the trees, and his pulse hurtled into his throat. Flashlights pierced through the night and swept along the ground about twenty feet ahead of them along the trail. Shadows shifted, closing in, and Finn picked up the pace. "Over here!"

Jonah Watson burst through the tree line with Chief Deputy Remi Barton directly behind him, their weapons raised. Watson took the lead, thick muscle threatening to break through the sleeves of his dark T-shirt. Blond hair cut through the intense blue gaze of the former FBI hazardous materials tech as he holstered his weapon and called over his shoulder, "Get an EMT!" His teammate closed the distance between them, arms out. "I can take her."

"She doesn't like to be touched." Finn shook him off, the tendons in his neck and shoulders straining, but he wouldn't go back on his word. Brushing past his team, he kept his hold tight around Camille as they parted to give him room. He wasn't leaving her. Not even at the expense of causing more damage to the wound in his side. He'd told her he'd get her out of there, and that was exactly what he intended to do. He'd already broken one promise to her. He wasn't about to break another.

"There's a body back there on the dock with three bullets in his chest." Mud suctioned at his heels, slowing him down, but the slight vibrations still rocking through his witness kept him moving. "Tell the EMTs she's losing blood from a wound in her shoulder. The suspect had a syringe full of clear liquid in his hand. I'm not sure if he injected her with anything. It still looked full when I kicked it out of his hand, but they need to know to run a tox screen when we get to the hospital."

"Reed, you need to put her down. You're losing blood faster than she is, and the more you push yourself, the more damage you could be causing." The slight rasp in Remi Barton's voice registered over the constant wall of rain in his ears. Her strong grip locked into his shoulder. "Finn, we can help—"

"I'm the reason he got to her in the first place. I promised her I'd protect her, and I didn't." One knee buckled out from under him, and he dropped. Small rocks and twigs bit into his kneecap. He'd already lost too much blood. He knew what his boss said was true, that Remi was trying to help, but that part of him that couldn't take anything less than hatred for not being there when Camille had been taken wouldn't let him release her. Tightening his hold on her, he bit back the scream trying to escape from his throat and put all of his weight into the leg that hadn't failed him.

But the strain was too much.

He didn't have anything else to give, and the hollowness he'd feared took control. The rain began to fall harder, as though it'd seen straight inside the darkest part of his mind and reflected the hopelessness coursing through him. He hadn't been strong enough to protect his mother that night. He wasn't strong enough to protect Camille now.

Two sets of hands threaded through the space between his arms and either side of his rib cage, Watson on one side and his chief deputy on the other. With his weight in their hands, Finn pushed to his feet and forced one foot in front of the other until he caught sight of the EMTs rushing to save his witness.

HER HEART WAS beating so fast, she thought it might burst through her chest. Sickness washed into her stomach, and she turned in the overheated bed as bile rose up her throat. Some kind of beeping ticked off to one side, in time with her pulse. She felt as though she was on the edge of a blade. Or had been stabbed with one.

Terror burned hot in her throat and eyes. She'd been abducted, tied to a chair, stabbed with the same piece of glass she'd tried to defend herself with. All because one killer wanted to use her as a prop in his sick mind game to outwit another. A bright blue bag appeared over her mouth a split second before the nausea took control.

"You're safe, Red. You're in Peace Harbor Medical Center," a familiar voice said. Warmth trickled down her spine at the sound of that voice. Steady. Real. Reliable. "You were under sedation so the doctor could take a look at the stab wound in your shoulder."

She clung to the rough, dirt-caked hand holding the bag over her mouth and nose, then brought her gaze up to the man positioned at the side of her bed. Finn. Blue eyes she'd come to rely on doubled in her vision before merging back into the handsome face of the marshal who'd saved her life. Again. A pitcher of water on the small table beside her bed claimed her attention. A hospital. She pointed to the cup weakly before attempting to roll into the center of her bed, but a sling around her left arm complicated what was supposed to be a seamless movement.

He poured her a cup of water and handed it to her, never taking his eyes from her.

Guarded emotion she couldn't read etched raw in his expression as cool water rushed down the back of her throat and cleared the bitter remnants of her stomach contents. "We really have to stop meeting like this."

"Did you think I was going to let you get away when you owe me an entire stash of mattress chocolate?" His smile shattered through the thin needle of fear spiking her blood pressure higher. He leaned back in his chair, grimacing as she had when the sling brushed against the wound in her shoulder, and she recognized the outline of padded dressing through the faded material of a superhero shirt she hadn't seen before. "I'm glad you're okay."

Violent memories coursed to the front of her mind. She'd cut herself loose with a piece of broken glass from a frame hanging in the houseboat. She'd rammed the makeshift weapon into her abductor's gut when he'd charged to attack. *I think this is the same exact spot I stabbed him before I left him to die.* Her breath hitched. Her fingers automatically sought the bed rail for balance as every second of being in her would-be killer's possession mixed with the demons of the past. The monitors to her left registered the uptick in her pulse. "He was telling the truth. He stabbed you. He—"

"Hey, look at me." Finn planted his hand over hers on the bed rail, but where her fight-or-flight instincts normally screamed to run, to hide, something inside wanted more. Wanted him, wanted the comfort he offered. "It was my own damn fault for leaving you in the house alone, but I'm still here, okay? We survived, and you're not getting rid of me that easily."

She nodded, taking a full breath to calm the rush of nerves lighting up her skin at his touch. "It wasn't your fault. I'm…some part of his plan to prove he's better than the Carver. Something about finishing the work Jeff Burnes didn't have the guts to." Anxiety churned through her. "I'm important to him, and I think he would've found me one way or another."

"You *were*," Finn said.

"What?" She didn't understand.

"You were part of his plan. The man who attacked you—Miles Darien, according to his fingerprints the ME pulled—is dead." He circled his thumb along the back of her hand, her skin heating and cooling in a hypnotic rhythm. "I shot him three times on that dock before he tried to inject you with a full syringe of succinylcholine. With that, he would've been able to sedate you within seconds so you wouldn't have the chance to fight back."

He reached for a file folder set on the same side table as the pitcher of water, then opened it and handed it to her.

The card stock felt as though it'd suck the life her attacker had left her with right out from her fingertips. She lowered her attention to the mug shot paper-clipped to some kind of report. Thick eyebrows arched over brown eyes in a straight line—the same eyes she'd memorized that had been framed by the ski mask covering his face. A shudder wracked through her from head to toe. Shiny blond hair framed a wide forehead, and his narrow jaw was peppered with matching stubble. If she didn't recognize the dead eyes staring straight into the camera that'd captured this mug shot, she'd believe Miles

Darien was anything but a killer. "I don't recognize his name. Miles Darien. He wasn't one of Jeff's— the Carver's—friends that I know of."

Would she ever be able to distance herself enough to call her ex-fiancé by the name he deserved and not the figment she'd known? Facing one serial killer had been enough to rattle her to her core. Facing a second threatened to throw her back to the beginning, to the ignorant woman she'd been before the Carver's attack. And she couldn't. She just couldn't.

She handed back the file and automatically tugged her hand into her chest to protect herself against the terror she'd felt while being held captive, but the sling wouldn't let her. She felt exposed, vulnerable, as the memories spiraled through her, and there was nothing she could do to stop them. "When I was in the houseboat, he told me he studied under the Carver for years, but I don't remember Jeff ever mentioning his name or him coming around."

"He can't hurt you anymore, Camille. He's gone." He was right. Finn had…shot a suspect to save her life. Killed him before her attacker had the opportunity to kill her. Camille didn't know what to say to that, didn't know what to think. No one had ever gone out of their way to protect her like that, to make sure she was the one who was standing at the end, and a strange surge of emotion braided with the loneliness she'd held on to for so long. Time stretched into a comfortable, warm fluid as his hand pressed over hers on the bed railing. The weight of his attention calmed the kaleidoscope of foreboding swirling inside. "Did Miles say anything else that you remember? Anything about Jodie Adler, how he managed to find you while you've been in witness protection or where the Carver might be?"

"He said he's not the one who killed her, that the Carver has been watching me." The monitor's incessant beeping accelerated with her rising pulse. Blood drummed in her ears. Air dragged slower through her lungs, and a terrible awareness began to sink in like a deadly poison. If it hadn't been for Finn, Miles Darien would've finished the job his mentor had started. "I don't know how he found me, and I don't know how he's connected to the Carver or how he knew about the photo I took of that clearing where Jodie Adler's body was found. All I know is he intended to use me as bait to show Jeff Burnes what he was capable of, that he almost succeeded, and I don't know what to do with that information. I've worked so hard to get my life back the way it was, but every step I've taken forward has been for nothing. This can't be it, Finn. This word carved into my skin was meant to constantly remind me how little control I actually have, that I'm just going to be a victim for the rest of my life. And they've won. They got exactly what they wanted."

In an instant, Finn hauled the bed railing into the lower position and stood. Hands sinking into the edge of the mattress, he leaned into her. Closer than he'd ever gotten before. "Camille, look at me. You didn't die out there. You survived, and now your attacker is the one who's going in the ground."

It wasn't enough. A humorless laugh escaped past her cracked lips. He didn't understand. How could he ever understand what she'd been through in the past year? He'd lost his mother to an armed fugitive and been shot in the process, but that man hadn't targeted Finn. The gunman hadn't tried to kill him. He'd been an innocent bystander. "I know what you're trying to do, and I appreciate it, but this is different than what you suffered as a kid."

"You're right. I'll never be in a position to tell you how to process your trauma, but you've earned some hard-won perspective." His voice softened, the lines etched around his eyes more shallow than a moment before. "You might see that branding as your greatest failure and have to deal with the repercussions for years to come, but I see them as proof that you're a survivor. The Carver and his protégé might've taken your passion for photography, your confidence and your sense of safety, but they didn't take your life, Red. No one can."

She lowered her gaze to the scratches and crusted blood on the back of her uninjured hand, then nodded. Despite following the suffocating rules to keep as much of the truth to herself as she could when she'd entered the witness-protection program, the marshal assigned to protect her had seen more than she'd originally estimated. He saw right through her, and the hole where a piece of her had been missing since the Carver's attack filled in slightly. Camille raised her gaze to meet his. "Thank you."

"Anytime." He slipped onto the edge of the mattress. "Now let's talk about the stash of chocolate you still owe me."

Tension bled from the tendons in her hands. "I knew you weren't going to let that go."

Chapter Ten

Finn shouldered inside the safe house, the automatic green emergency lights flickering. He tightened his grip around the handle of Camille's overnight bag as she moved past him, the discomfort in his side renewed. It'd been a clean cut. No infection. No major damage. Although he couldn't help but enjoy the fact that the bastard who'd stabbed him had left this world in a lot more pain.

He closed the door behind him and secured the dead bolts. Armed the security system. Less than twenty-four hours ago this place had felt like a reprieve from the world. Now he couldn't help but see it as more of a shelter from the storm. With the Carver's protégé in the morgue, Finn had no doubt the master would show his face, and that meant doing what he should've done in the first place: keep Camille safe until her former fiancé was back in federal custody. "I'll get you something to eat while you clean up."

She moved down the long hallway toward the main room but stopped at the end. The strap of the shoulder sling seemed to dig into the tendon between her neck and shoulder. Long red hair trailed down her back in clumped strings, and an instant flash flood of memory rushed to the front of his mind. Her lying on that dock, her abductor standing right over her. If he'd been there mere seconds later, would she have survived? Would he have found her? Camille lifted her uninjured arm across her chest, then dropped it to her side, as though she'd realized she couldn't cross her arms with the sling in place. "I'm not…I'm not hungry."

"Okay." He followed her path along the hallway and set her overnight bag on the floor. An overwhelming feeling of helplessness dug deep into the space he'd kept reserved for the memories of the night he'd lost his mother and threatened to expose that emptiness to the world. Camille had been taken because of him. She'd nearly died out there because he hadn't been strong enough to protect her. "Is there anything else I can get you?"

She turned toward him, the hollows under her eyes more pronounced than they'd been at the hospital. Exhaustion clung to the weariness that seemingly pulled her toward the floor. "Do you have a time machine?"

"Unfortunately, no, but if I did, I'd sign it over to you," he said.

"In that case, you can tell me how you plan to find Jeff Burnes. I want to know what the US Marshals Service is doing to track down the Carver before he has another chance to kill me." She waved her hand toward the wall, the sleeves of the long cardigan sweater she wore overtaking her wrists and palms. "Directly or indirectly. I know I'm not a police officer or someone who they'll give access to concerning the investigation, but I just… I need to know."

Indirectly. She was referring to Miles Darien, the Carver's protégé. Though from the sound of it, Miles had been working on his own to use Camille as proof of power to his master. There were no indications the Carver had been in touch with Miles during his imprisonment or the past five days of freedom. No inexplicable calls in Miles's cell-phone records. No digital transfers or a trail of cash withdrawn from her attacker's account that would help the veteran killer during his time as a fugitive. From the evidence Florence PD had recovered, it didn't look like Miles Darien had contact with his mentor at all, and the only thing Jeff Burnes had been given access to in federal custody had been a copy of the *Chicago Tribune* each morning. No visitors. No phone calls. No mail.

"Fair enough." He had to be honest with her. She

deserved the truth. All of it. Finn leaned against the wall beside him. "Authorities have no idea where he is, not even a general idea. It seems the day Jeff Burnes escaped custody is the day he dropped off the face of the planet. We have BOLOs sent to every law-enforcement agency in the country and every marshal the department of justice employs looking for him. We're reinterviewing victims' families, your former coworkers, anybody who's been connected to Jeff Burnes over the past five years. So far, that hasn't turned up any new leads. The only thing we have is a possible connection between him and Miles Darien, thanks to your statement and his body in the morgue, but we're still trying to prove they knew each other. Working in the governor's office in Chicago would've given Miles direct access to details about your case, including those Chicago PD and the FBI had intentionally left out of the media. He could've just been trying to convince you he was the Carver's protégé and confidant in order to make himself look better or to get Jeff Burnes's attention through copycatting. Or maybe they really do have a relationship, and we haven't seen it yet."

"What do you believe?" She stared up at him as though the foundation of her entire world depended on him answering that question. Like she needed him to believe Miles Darien was, in fact, connected to her ex-fiancé, that the Carver was still out there targeting her, waiting for her to make a mistake. But the truth was, there were too many pieces of this puzzle missing for him to come to a conclusion.

"I believe in evidence and having all the facts. We've got two victims recovered from out in those woods, both of which have been confirmed as homicide through strangulation. Miles Darien attacked you twice with the same MO as the Carver, but in a different order, and your therapist, Dr. Henry Gruner, has alibis for both attacks on you and for the time Jodie Adler was killed." A sinking sensation pooled in his gut. As of right now, the investigation behind these attacks was at a dead end. "Dr. Gruner might've been privy to the time and place you took that photograph, but he also filed a police report with Florence PD that his office had been broken into a couple weeks after that particular session of yours with him. I reviewed the report. His office had been trashed, his desk drawers rifled through. He kept his patient notes in a notebook taped to the underside of his desk, and somehow whoever'd broken in found them. His statement said that particular notebook was filled with both yours and Jodie Adler's session notes, along with two other patients. We've got the names of the other women and details watching their houses in case this doesn't end with Miles Darien." Finn pushed away from the wall and stepped toward her. "I believe you've been through a lot these past few days, and that there's nothing we can do to change any of it tonight."

She lowered her gaze to the floor, disappointment clear in her expression. "You're saying Miles probably lied to me about not killing Jodie Adler. He just wanted to get inside my head, to see if the possibility of the Carver closing in would increase my fear."

"Manipulation is a cornerstone of psychopathic behavior. I'm sure it wasn't the first time he got satisfaction from messing with his prey." Though they hadn't found any other missing victims in the area matching Jodie Adler's or Camille's appearances. Finn studied the changes in her expression, tried to read past the rigid guard she kept in place, but she'd gotten damn good at throwing up those walls she believed kept her safe from getting hurt. "Deputy Watson sent over Miles Darien's autopsy report a little while ago. His DNA and fingerprints came back tied to a cold case that occurred back in Chicago last year. A female deputy US marshal who'd been bound, carved with the word *mine* on her chest and strangled. The FBI profilers believe that was his first kill. The Carver had been arrested a few weeks before, you'd been relocated and Miles Darien saw an opening to fill, a chance to make a name for himself before he decided to finish Jeff Burnes's work with you."

"Is that how he found me? Through the marshal?

You're saying they didn't connect him to the case, even with fingerprints and DNA?" she asked. "Were they waiting for him to show up to the police station with a sign around his neck that said he was a murderer?"

"Records show the marshal logged on to the Warrant Information Network two hours after the Chicago investigators recovered her body in March. Just over a month after you'd been relocated to Florence." Her frustration resonated through him, a violin string strung too tight and ready to snap. "As for tying him to the murder, neither Miles Darien's fingerprints nor his DNA were in the system. Until now."

The delicate muscles along her throat corded as she swallowed. "And the remains you found, the bones in the woods… Do you know who they belong to?"

"No ID yet," he said. "But the medical examiner put time of death around a year ago. It's impossible to get an exact date, but based on insect activity, weather conditions and the decomposition of his clothing and body tissues, she's sure the victim was killed toward the end of February of last year. We wouldn't have connected the investigations if it weren't for the fact there was evidence of strangulation. Too much of a coincidence considering we found Jodie Adler's body not far from where he'd been killed, and the fact you'd been relocated less than a quarter mile from the scene."

"If he was killed in February, then Miles Darien couldn't have killed him." Her fingers played with the hem of her sweater, as though she needed the comfort, and it felt like the gravity holding him in place had vanished. "He was still in Chicago, targeting that marshal."

Finn narrowed his attention on her. "You're right. With Jeff Burnes still in federal custody and Miles Darien occupied in Chicago, there's no way either of them could've killed that victim around the time the medical examiner reported."

Which meant the ME had gotten the timeline wrong, or there was a possibility the two homicides—Jodie Adler's and their latest victim—weren't connected. Only the MO and location said otherwise. Or had the US Marshals Service had the wrong suspect all along? A headache pulsed at the base of his skull. As a law-enforcement officer who went the extra mile in anticipating and preparing himself for every threat possible, this case pushed at his physical and mental limits like no other. Miles Darien was dead, but the Carver was still out there. Could there be another player in this dark, twisted game they hadn't seen yet?

"Finn." Her voice softened with the release of the tension around her collarbone. "I don't know who's behind this, but something is telling me they aren't going to stop until they get what they want, and that scares me to death." She stepped into him, notched her chin higher to stare up, and a sudden awareness of Camille's proximity hit. Her tongue darted out from between her lips. "The only time I've felt safe these past few days is with you. You're the only one I can trust. So will you…will you hold me while I fall asleep? Please."

He closed the few inches of space between them and slipped his arms around her until her ear rested against his chest. Right where she belonged. Smoothing down her frizzed hair, he set his cheek on the crown of her head. "I'll hold you as long as you want."

"Okay." That single word vibrated through him and settled in the empty space behind his sternum, a missing piece that'd been hurting for a long time. "But to be clear, I don't mean here in the middle of the floor."

A SOFT THUMP pounded in the palm of her uninjured hand. Drugging sleep urged her to keep her eyes closed for a few more minutes of oblivion, but she couldn't ignore the beard tickling the bridge of her nose anymore. The slow rise and fall of the muscled chest under her urged Camille to open her eyes, and the intoxicating scent of soap and laundry filled her lungs. Finn.

Strong arms secured her against him, and she didn't dare move. The pads of her fingertips registered every beat of his heart under her hand. Strong, reliable. Safe. Straightening her finger, she traced the outline of his jaw through thick hair. It was softer than she'd imagined. Like the vintage feel of his latest superhero T-shirt. Seconds slipped by, maybe a minute. She didn't care. The past three days had been filled with nothing but fear, running and pain, but in this moment, with him, it seemed as though nothing could hurt her.

You might see that branding as your greatest failure and have to deal with the repercussions for years to come, but I see them as proof that you're a survivor. His words from the hospital echoed over and over in her head. She hadn't given him enough credit. Finn might never understand what it was like to be in her exact position, but he did understand hurt. He understood grief for a life he'd never see again. There was nothing he could do to bring back his mother, but Camille had a choice. She could let the Carver and his protégé, Miles Darien, haunt her for the rest of her life. Or she could take it back, take control again.

She rested her hand on his chest. He stirred under her touch but didn't wake as she maneuvered out from between his arms and pressed to sit up with her uninjured hand. The comforter he'd dragged over them pooled at her waist, and she set her bare feet on the floor. Aches and bruising pain urged her to climb back in that bed, to rest, but the tingling spreading through her fingers wouldn't let up. She crossed the short distance to the bathroom and swung the door partially closed behind her, enough to gain access to the small walk-in closet positioned behind it.

There was no hesitation this time. No self-doubt. No images of the Carver's victims clawing to the surface. They hadn't survived Jeff's sick obsession, but she had. As much as she hated the idea that all those women would never get the chance to live out the rest of their lives, she couldn't waste another moment trying to live one that didn't exist anymore.

Camille reached for the camera bag Finn had stashed on one of the closet shelves and tugged the zipper around the curve of the canvas. Dim bathroom lighting reflected off the cracked LCD monitor then vanished in an outline of her hand as she pulled the heavy device from its casing. Holding the camera close to her chest, she felt the muscles in her arm immediately engage to counter the familiar and comfortable weight. She exhaled softly, her thumb positioned against the power slide. She turned it on.

The camera almost seemed to sigh with the surge of power, a high-pitched ringing reaching her ears. She clutched one edge of the device in her unin-

jured hand, then used her opposite hand to remove
the cap protecting the lens. The tingling in her fingers surged down her legs, carrying her back into
the main room of the safe house. Emergency green
lighting cast shadows across the marshal still asleep
in the bed. It'd been scientifically proven that observ-
ing a moment through a camera lens increased the
brain's chance of forgetting those seconds forever.
She stopped at the end of the bed. Right then, she
just had to commit the sight of him to memory, as
she'd done with so many other important moments
throughout her career as a photographer. Her fighter.
Her protector. Her hero.

Camille raised the camera and compressed the
shutter release button.

The camera clicked with a soft hiss.

Angling the lens down, she studied the LCD
monitor, searching for her next breath. One second
stretched into the next as her entire nervous system
seemed to relax, and a sense of right filled her.

This. This was what she'd missed.

A camera in her hand, the feeling of alignment
in her soul. She couldn't explain the addictive sen-
sations coursing through her veins, but she didn't
have to. She only had to feel, to let the nightmares
and pain that'd taken her passion be buried by the
roar of newfound excitement. Camille rounded the
end of the bed and set one knee near Finn's feet, then

raised the viewfinder to her eye. Another click of the shutter release. Absolutely perfect. The subject of this new wave of freedom cracked open his eyes, a closed-lipped smile stretching his mouth, and her gut clenched with a sudden overwhelming desire. For this moment. For him.

"I see you've found your camera." Interlacing his fingers behind his head, Finn took complete control of her attention. The pins and needles in her hands exploded throughout her whole body at the sight of him so relaxed, so confident. Wide shoulders spread across his pillow, his muscled frame clearly outlined through his latest superhero T-shirt and sweats, and her tongue hit the roof of her mouth. "It's going to take a lot of editing to make me look like one of your Antarctic landscapes, though."

"You're perfect the way you are." Genuine laughter bubbled from her as she balanced her weight on the edge of the mattress. A thread of thrill wound through her. He'd studied her work. Of course, he had. He'd said so himself. Whenever he took on a new witness-protection assignment, he researched every detail of the person he was protecting in order to see the next threat coming. But knowing she'd been a photographer and making that extra effort to study her work were two different things. She raised her camera and took another shot. And she paused. She hadn't *been* a photographer. She *was* one, would always be one. Because Finn had shown her no matter what happened, photography was part of her, and that was something nobody could take. Not even the Carver. The wound in her shoulder burned with the added weight of her camera, but she pushed it to the back of her mind. No. Her would-be killer didn't get to be part of this moment. As far as she was concerned, nothing existed outside of this room. It was just her, Finn and her camera. "Editing would only ruin the rawness of what I'm feeling."

He pushed upright, the heaviness of those brilliant blue eyes never leaving her even though the pain in his side must be gutting him from the inside. "You're an amazing woman, Camille. I've never known anyone to not only survive what you've been through, but to also come out on the other side braver and more determined than ever. Not even me."

Heat flooded up her neck and into her cheeks. She studied the last photo she'd taken in the LCD monitor, not really focusing on anything in particular. A distraction from looking at what she really wanted. Him. The muscles at one corner of her mouth quirked, but one compliment didn't mean anything. Certainly not him flirting. They had their assigned roles. She was his witness. He was her protector. Anything more wasn't possible because of his intention never to go through what he had when he'd lost his mom again. He never wanted to love another person so much, because the mere thought of losing them broke something inside. No matter how many times she'd imagined reaching out for him, she wouldn't. She craved connection, emotional fullness, to counter the loneliness she'd been forced to swallow, and Finnick Reed had made it his single goal in life to never get attached to anyone again. Anything that happened between them would be superficial—a lie—and she'd always need more than that. "Careful, Marshal Reed, you keep buttering me up like that and I'll start to think you might actually care about me."

"I do." He climbed to his knees, the dip in the mattress tugging at her balance. Pulling her closer to him. Her heart jerked in her chest as Finn slowly took the camera from her hands and set it up near her pillow, leaving nothing for her to hide behind but the shirt she'd borrowed from him. Frenzied responsiveness mixed with a hint of panic tightened her throat as he slid one hand under her elbow, then the other. He moved slower than he needed to, giving her the chance to flee, but over the past few days, Finn had become the anchor keeping her in the moment. Not the past. "Of all the witnesses I've been assigned to protect, of all the women who've marched in and out of my life, I've never wanted any of them more than I've wanted you. You're the most honest, determined and strongest woman I've met, and the only one who makes me think moving on from what happened to my mother all those years ago is possible. You're the example I want to live up to, Red, and there's nothing more I want to do than kiss the hell out of you right now, but if you're not ready, or you don't feel the same—"

"I'm ready." Surprise stole the oxygen from her lungs. She was? Camille lowered her gaze to where his bare palms rested under her elbows, his body heat bleeding through the fabric of her sling, and she let her hand rest against his arm. Instant desire coiled low in her belly. Hell yes, she was ready. Not just for anyone—she was ready for him. Ready to experience this crazed fascination and desire for Finn Reed just once. It wouldn't last beyond his protection detail, she knew that, but she wouldn't live the rest of her life wondering what could've happened if she'd been more open, more honest about what she wanted.

She pressed her mouth to his, framing his bristled jaw with her uninjured hand, and that same sense of alignment she'd felt with a camera in her hand exploded behind her rib cage. Her soul caught fire deep inside as he swept his tongue past the seam of her lips, and then she was falling.

Chapter Eleven

The smooth skin of Camille's arm pressed against his uninjured side as she slowly whisked thick chocolate batter into the only mixing bowl he could find in the place. He wasn't sure how long she'd kissed him—mere minutes, maybe an eternity—before their stomachs had audibly protested against the adrenaline-fueled days they'd fought through. She'd pulled away with a deep laugh he hadn't been able to get out of his mind, and was now consuming herself with creating a monstrous dessert sure to make them sick.

"I didn't realize there was such a thing as jumbo brownies." He cracked another egg into the bowl for her, then tossed the shell into the sink on the other side of the kitchen. The space wasn't ideal for cooking, but it certainly appeased the heat that'd been building since Camille had taken his photograph. At that moment, poised above him with the camera in her hand, she'd been everything he'd imagined her before the Carver's attack had stolen her life. She'd been free—happy, even—and he hadn't been able to look away.

Finn reached for her and brushed a streak of cocoa powder from her upper lip with his index finger. Every second she'd allowed him into her personal space had been worth the pain pulsing in his side. He eyed the empty boxes of baking mix, spots of oil and bits of eggshells discarded on the counter, and at that moment, he felt more anchored than he had his entire life. Uncertainty fled down through his legs, the nightmare of this case instantly forgotten. Because of Camille. Because of the way she'd chosen to get her life back, to push past being a victim and become a survivor stronger than he'd ever imagined. Because of the way she'd taken control from her attackers. Hell, the woman was inspiring. "You had some cocoa powder on your mouth."

Her smile lit up his insides.

"Any dessert can be labeled jumbo if you're willing to ignore the amount of sugar in each serving, which I'm great at." Pinning the bowl between her wrist in the sling and her stomach, she struggled to keep a grip around the ceramic while combining the ingredients. Lean muscle flexed with each scrape of the whisk against the side of the bowl, but her attention had slid to him. Satisfaction tugged at his mouth a split second before the bowl fell out of her hold and hit the counter, flinging brownie batter into the air.

Cold, wet mix plastered to one side of his face and mouth. He closed his eyes as a large glob pancaked into his eyebrow. It dripped down his neck, onto his shirt then hit the counter, but from what he could tell when he'd swiped it away and opened his eyes to assess the damage, he'd gotten the least of it.

Her long, red hair was streaked with lumps of brown semibeaten brownie batter. She swiped her hair out of her face with her wrist then stared up at him with nothing but seriousness in her expression. "How about now? Do I have anything on my face now?"

Laughter bellowed past his lips. He reached out and swiped a splotch dripping from her cheek with his thumb, then brought the batter to his mouth. Sweet chocolate spread across his tongue. Her gaze centered on his movements, her big green-blue eyes wide, and that deep warmth he'd reveled in when she'd kissed him pushed past his control. "Nothing a good shower can't take care of I'm sure."

"Is—is that supposed to be an invitation?" Her voice held a note of wonder, as though she hadn't possibly considered the idea of anything more between them than the single kiss they'd shared, however explosive it might've been on his end. The air between them grew thick, and his natural instincts warned him to back away. He hadn't met anyone like her. Never would. She was unique in her honesty, her creative side, her self-awareness, and with nothing to hide. She'd beaten the odds of survival not once, but three separate times. She was everything he wasn't and everything he hadn't realized he'd needed to move on from the past. With Camille, he wouldn't have a reason to look back. Only forward. And that scared the hell out of him.

But as much as he wanted to give in to his own selfish desire, he wouldn't push her to offer anything more than she was willing to give up freely. She'd spent the last year afraid for her life, afraid of everyone around her. Reading into interactions, trying to uncover strangers' true intentions. Paranoid. Of all the people who'd failed her over the last year, he wanted to be the one she could feel comfortable with, to be the one she trusted. No matter the situation, she needed someone she could rely on, and he couldn't be that for her once this investigation closed. Finn turned into her. "How about I finish up these brownies while you clean up? That way, by the time you're finished in the shower, we can put on a movie and dig in together."

"That sounds perfect." A relieved smile spread her lips thin as she raised her hand to his face and pulled another glob of batter from his beard, then disappeared into the bathroom. The sound of water pelting tile filled his ears.

Within a few minutes, he'd sectioned what was left of the brownie batter, managed to get the baking sheet into the too-small oven and used a kitchen towel to sweep most of the mess into the sink. A humorless laugh rumbled through his chest as he stared at the splotches of dried brownie mix on the back of his hand. Hell. The void in the pit of his gut didn't seem to hurt as much now. He felt it clear down to... Well, everywhere. Such a simple thing, helping Camille make brownies. Seemed from the time he'd been ten years old he'd been running, avoiding having to think about anything more than the problem right in front of him. He'd hated the thought of not having a case to chase or a fugitive to hunt. Sitting still, in the silence, had been an invitation for everything he hadn't wanted to think about. And right now, locked inside this safe house while the rest of his team tracked down leads and ran the investigation, there was only Camille. He might not have set out to expand on his baking skills with her today, but he'd been willing. It'd mattered to her, a distraction from the nightmare waiting outside these walls, and he had to admit it'd forced him to focus on something other than the next investigation, the next witness he'd be assigned to protect, the next threat. When was the last time he'd slowed down long enough to enjoy the moment? Or had he ever?

The muffled noise of the shower cut off at the same time the oven timer screamed from behind, and Finn was shoved back into reality. He swept the last of the eggshells into the sink and pulled the hot baking sheet from the oven. Melted chocolate mixed with the aroma of peanut butter in his lungs but failed to erase the hint of lavender clinging to his shirt. He had a feeling nothing would. Finn brushed his palms against his jeans and rounded the counter for the tablet he'd packed in his duffel bag. The bathroom door swung inward, and he slowed. "Hey."

"My stomach growled the entire time I was in the shower from the smell of the brownies baking." Head cocked to one side, she towel-dried her hair as she moved into the main room, careful of her injured shoulder. He found himself captivated by the way her fingers combed through her hair. By the darkness of each water stain spotting one of his older superhero T-shirts along her collarbone and how she'd forgone thick sweats in favor of sleep shorts that showed off the smoothness and bruising along her legs. "I'm starving."

So was he, and not for the dessert they'd made together.

"I just pulled them out. I was about to find a movie on my tablet." His fingers curled up into his palms as every cell in his body honed in on the curves of her soft frame beneath his shirt. Finn forced himself to unpack the tablet from his bag—anything to keep his mind off the sudden aching heaviness in his legs. He stood, using every last ounce of strength he had left to unlock the device. "What do you feel like watching?"

"Doesn't matter. I doubt I'm going to be able to pay much attention to it, anyway, with the promise of chocolate and my very own bodyguard sitting next to me." Her voice sounded closer than it should have, and he turned to face her. She'd closed the distance between them, the towel still in her hand. It slipped from her fingers, pooling at her feet as she framed his jaw between her hands and pressed her mouth against his. Her kiss was hot, hungry, with desperation in the sweep of her tongue past his lips, and he matched her stroke for stroke in an attempt to cool the raging fire inside. In vain. No matter how much of herself Camille offered to him, it'd never be enough. Not in this lifetime. She pulled back slightly, then whispered against his mouth. "It really is a shame the only place to sit and watch a movie is the bed."

He dropped to weave his arms behind her knees and back and lifted her into him. Her laugh drowned the pain in his side as he headed toward the kitchen counter. Three steps. Four. She was right. No point in wasting all that hard work. He nodded toward the baking sheet, which had had enough time to cool since he'd pulled it from the oven. "Such a shame."

She curled long fingers around the edges of the baking sheet and held on as he carried her across the small space toward the bed. She'd tasted of honey before, but he couldn't wait to find out how much more addictive she might become with all that chocolate and peanut butter added into the mix.

"I DON'T THINK I'll ever see brownies as an innocent dessert again," he said.

Her laugh shook through her. Camille traced the curve of the muscles across his bare abdomen with her finger. She loved touching him, feeling his heart beneath her hand. It proved this wasn't a dream. That she was alive when the world had set out to smother her. There were still patches of chocolate sticking to her fingers, but all she could focus on right now was how…right the past couple of hours had felt.

She'd given Finn access to the hidden, untouched parts of her—inside and out—for the first time since she'd discovered who her fiancé really was, but despite the fact Finn could hold that power over her, she didn't feel vulnerable. Not with him. The regrets, the guilt, the fear, the expectations she'd set on herself—all of those things had disappeared the moment she'd made the choice that what she wanted mattered. That she'd wanted him. The only way to get her life back was to take the responsibility into her own hands, and that was exactly what she'd done. "We'll have to keep that particular combination in mind next time."

"Next time?" He notched his chin down in order to look at her, every inch of him the man she'd imagined under those superhero shirts he wore. "If that's the case, I'm going to have to invest in more sheets after this."

Battle-earned aches replaced the deep pleasure he'd brought out of her body. Pain streaked through her opposite shoulder and the back of her head, but she'd left the pain medication script her surgeon had ripped from his prescription pad unfilled for fear of falling back into the numbing habits she'd held on to for so long. Instead, surprise slowed the path of her finger across his stomach. He wasn't backing away from this connection they'd forged together. He wasn't discarding this as a mistake he could walk away from when the investigation was over and the Carver was back behind bars. There'd been more to it than a casual way to past the time. At least, for her. She'd given him something she hadn't given to anyone else, hadn't even thought of surrendering, and he was acting as if it'd meant as much to him as it had to her. "Unless you have other plans that don't include a bed."

"I might." His smooth smile knocked the uncertainty swirling through her down a peg. Finn planted his mouth against her forehead, then set his chin against the top of her head. "The place isn't that big, but I'm a creative guy, and I'm fairly certain that shower is large enough for two people. Although you're the only woman I've brought here."

Unease bled from the muscles along her spine.

"No other witnesses you've seduced?" She had no right to ask, but part of her—the part that'd started hoping for this bond built on ridiculous inside jokes and their combined love of mattress chocolate—needed to know. "No other women waiting for you to get reassigned from this case?"

"Women? No," he said. "Not unless you count my boss."

She closed her eyes, digging one corner of the gauze taped to his side under her thumbnail. She wasn't sure how long they'd been lying there, simply savoring the feel of one another in stillness, but Camille didn't dare break the spell. Not yet. The investigation, the fugitive still out there, the past—none of it mattered right then, and not for the first time since he'd saved her life, she could breathe a bit easier. She was safe here. With him. She'd always be safe as long as he was next to her.

Sliding her jaw along his shoulder, she stared up at him, her bare skin pressed against him. "I think your mom would be proud of you, of how brave you were out there in those woods. You might wear superhero shirts because that was the last gift she gave you before she died, but you're as much of a hero as any one of those characters on your chest."

"I've told you before. I'm not a hero, Red." He pushed out of the bed, leaving her cold under the sheets. Reaching for his pants, he threaded his feet into the legs and secured them around his waist. He clenched his shirt in his hands—another superhero shirt, but she hadn't recognized the logo—and the veins in his arm seemed to be fighting to break through his skin. "A hero wouldn't have given Miles Darien the chance to take you in the first place. A hero never would've left you in that house alone or gotten stabbed in the process of searching for his witness."

"It was my fault then that Miles Darien got a hold of me?" She slid her feet to the floor, the sheet clutched around her. "It's my fault the Carver is out there, most likely planning his next move to finish what he started a year ago?"

"What?" The deep lines between his eyebrows eased, and the deputy US marshal she'd relied on for so long—the man she wanted to keep relying on when this case was finished—returned. "Of course not."

"If I'd recognized Jeff Burnes for what he was sooner, maybe I would've been able to save more of his victims. If I'd only been stronger, he couldn't have taken my love for my photography," she said.

"If I'd known about Miles Darien before he took me from the house, Florence PD wouldn't have found Jodie Adler's body out there in those woods."

He tossed his shirt to the bed then scrubbed a hand down his face. His beard bristled in the silence between them as her words seemed to sink in, and the fight drained out of him. "Camille, none of that is on you."

"You see how ridiculous it sounds, then? To take the blame for something you had no control over? Those are the exact thoughts I've lived with for the past year, Finn. My fantasy self—this woman I've built in my head and aspire to become—doesn't let them bother her, but the real me? That guilt? It's eaten at me every day since I walked away from the Carver's attack, making me question why I was the only one who survived. But you showed me even though I'm at the center of this puzzle, I'm not the only piece." She moved around the bed, closing the distance between them. "Heroes aren't given their status because they prevent the bad things from happening. It's because they will do anything to stand up to the people responsible, and that's what you've done for me." She set her hand on his arm. "Miles Darien wanted to prove he was stronger than the Carver, a man who'd already taken so much of my life without killing me. I was integral to his plan to do that. There was nothing you could've done to stop him, and internalizing that guilt for what happened will only leave you with a numbness that will contaminate every aspect of your life and take away the things you love about yourself. So you're my hero, Finn, whether you want to hear it or not. When you let the numbness and guilt win, there's nothing you won't do to hear someone say they believe in and care about you."

Surprise brightened the color of his eyes. "You just said you care about me."

"Don't let it go to your head." She set her fists against his chest, still clutching the sheet around her. "I tell that to all the law-enforcement officers who've been assigned to protect me over the past year. You'd be surprised at how easily I deflected the FBI's suspicion when I cozied up to the special agent in charge on the case."

"I'll remember that." He leaned down and swept his mouth across hers. Just the simple action, the gentleness, resurrected the tingling sensation usually isolated in her fingers and hands when she held her camera and pushed it through her entire body. She couldn't remember the last time she'd felt so… important to another person. Significant. He curved his hands around her hips and seized the sheet covering her from chest to toes. "I've got brownie in places I've never imagined food to ever end up, so how about I change these sheets and my clothes, and we eat something unsexy enough to bring down our blood sugar?"

"Who said we need clothes for that?" A wave of electricity and daring she'd never felt before burned through her, and she couldn't help but revel in the newfound confidence.

The shrill sound of Finn's phone from the night-stand beside the bed burst the bubble they'd created around themselves, and Camille flinched against the onslaught of reality. They might've had the past couple of hours to themselves, but they couldn't ignore the real world forever. Not with the Carver still out there.

"Hold on to that thought." Finn unwrapped himself from around her and went for the phone, catching it on the fourth ring before the caller was sent to voice mail. "Reed."

She rounded back around the bed as Finn disappeared down the hallway toward the front door and reached for her camera, which she'd placed on the nightstand. She could hear his mumbled conversation, but she only had attention for the sleek curves of the instrument that'd brought her passion to life. Not much had changed over the past few hours, since she'd taken those photos, and yet there'd been a major shift inside of her.

Flipping the power switch, she queued the last few photos onto the LCD monitor. Finn, in all his glory, stretched across the bed, completely oblivious to the lens and the woman behind it. She'd struggled every second of every day to simply compress the shutter release button before Jodie Adler's body had been found in the clearing. She'd hadn't seen an end date to the terror that'd kept her from rediscovering her art. Not until Finn had given her a safe place to confront her internal demons—not just physically, in the safe house, but emotionally. If it hadn't been for him reminding her how to feel, to trust someone other than herself, she'd have stayed buried in the thick, black haze that'd taken control of her life forever.

She brushed her thumb across the screen, following the outline of his face, his mouth and the length of his throat. She'd meant what she'd said before. He was a hero—not only to her, but also to all of the witnesses he'd protected up to this point—and because of that, she'd fallen in love with him. She'd fallen for the deputy US marshal determined never to let himself care about someone else for fear they'd be taken from him, as his mother had been. But he cared about her, didn't he? He'd battled through the pain of being stabbed, of losing blood, of putting himself at risk to find her when Miles Darien had come so close to killing her. He'd gone out of his way to respect the personal distance she'd needed. He'd put her needs above his own, cooked for her, comforted her, placed himself between the threat outside that front door and where she'd slept. That had to mean something more than his usual feelings toward those other witnesses he'd been assigned to protect in the past.

Footsteps padded behind her, but she didn't have to turn around to know Finn had ended his call. Camille switched off the camera and replaced it on the nightstand. She hadn't felt exposed lying next to him in the bed with nothing coming between their bodies a few minutes ago, but she couldn't help but feel the sheet provided little protection against the nervousness pimpling her skin now. She'd kept her feelings and thoughts to herself in the past, but she wasn't that woman anymore. She didn't want to be that woman anymore. She wanted to be what he'd described back in the hospital, the woman she'd fantasized of becoming all her life. Not a victim but a survivor, and that meant she couldn't hide behind the mask she'd put in place after losing everything twelve months ago. "Finn, there's something we need to talk about—"

"The medical examiner identified the remains I found in the woods." His chest stretched wide, the muscles bunching and relaxing with every breath. He clutched his phone in his hand a little too tightly, bones white under the rough skin of his knuckles. "Dental records and bone marrow tests confirmed it a little while ago. The skeleton I found belongs to Dr. Henry Gruner."

Chapter Twelve

The color drained from her face.

"What? No." Camille shook her head. She stumbled back as though she'd taken a punch to the gut, and the last few hours of bliss they'd created together dissipated. "That's not…that's not possible. Those can't be Dr. Gruner's remains you found. He didn't die a year ago because I've been seeing him as a patient all this time. He's been helping me process everything that's happened since I came to Oregon."

Finn planted his feet in place, giving her the space she needed to hear the truth. "The medical examiner confirmed it. I asked her to run the tests again, but dental records and DNA don't lie, Camille. Someone killed the real Dr. Gruner a year ago with the Carver's MO, left him out in those woods and has assumed his identity. The man you've been seeing is a fraud."

"None of this makes sense." Her gaze fell to a distant point past his left hip, and the stab wound in his side flared with awareness. She clenched her hands at her side, suddenly seeming so much smaller than she had a few minutes ago. Turning back toward the bed, she discarded the sheet she'd been clutching around her and reached for her clothes. Within seconds, she'd slipped perfect legs into a pair of fresh jeans and wound her injured shoulder into an oversize sweater from her overnight bag. She maneuvered around the end of the bed barefoot. "The only man I know who is intelligent enough, driven enough and deranged enough to kill a psychologist and assume his identity—to do all of this—escaped prison less than a week ago."

She'd read his mind. "It's possible Miles Darien wasn't the Carver's only protégé. He could've recruited someone else to finish his work while he was waiting for trial, or he had a bigger fan base than the feds originally believed. There are plenty of copycats out there waiting to make a name for themselves, or hell, even to carry on a killer's work without revealing themselves. They do it to increase the public's panic, cast doubt on an ongoing trial or to get the killer's attention." He shifted his weight between both feet. "Can you think of anybody Jeff Burnes mentioned in conversation or someone who came around the apartment leading up to the first attack in

Chicago? Anyone who seemed particularly interested in you before you were put in witness protection?"

"No. I told the FBI everything I remembered in the weeks before Jeff attacked me. We worked with a lot of the same people. Producers, editors, other photographers and writers, but they were all interviewed and alibied before I was put in the program." She bit her bottom lip, the small muscles in her cheeks twitching. Her aquamarine eyes raised to meet his, and the confidence, the fire, that'd been there when they'd made love drained away. "I don't understand why this is happening, Finn. How someone could insert themselves into my life, pretend to care about me, claim to love me and that they want to spend the rest of their life with me, all for the purpose of killing me in the end? What kind of person does that? What kind of person recruits others to inflict the same kind of pain on countless other victims?"

A strange surge of guilt braided with hot anger for the SOB who'd convinced her to trust him then ripped apart her world. Blood drummed in his ears. He didn't have an answer for her, couldn't begin to imagine the confusion and fear tearing at all the good memories she'd made over the past year. One thing he did know—he couldn't keep his distance anymore. Taking her hands in his, he smoothed his fingers along her wrist, then higher along her triceps, careful of her injured shoulder. He stepped into her, following the curve of her shoulder blades, and hugged her close. The hint of lavender in her hair urged his racing heart into calmness, despite the churn of anxiety for her safety. "I don't know, but we're going to figure it out. I promise."

Someone had followed her to Oregon, predicted her need for psychological support after the Carver's failed attack, killed the only therapist in Florence who specialized in trauma recovery with a known killer's MO and assumed a man's entire life as his own. Only it couldn't have been the Carver. Not according to the warden or the guards of MCC Chicago, not to mention Burnes's cell mate. The bastard might still be on the run after escaping federal custody, but Finn honestly couldn't place Camille's ex in the silhouette of the man psychologically tormenting her now. The timeline didn't add up.

"You're going to get through this, Red. It's not going to be easy. Some days will be harder than others, and there will be times you'll want to give up. There's going to be nightmares and triggers, but you're stronger than all of it. I know you are. You've survived what most people don't three times now. It has nothing to do with your fantasy self or luck. It's your determination to keep what happened to you from happening to others." Her exhales warmed his neck, kept him in the moment as that scared ten-year-old kid he'd been stepped into power in his head.

"Healing doesn't mean the damage never existed. It just means the past doesn't control your life anymore, and you owe it to yourself to move on. Here in Oregon, back in Chicago, wherever you decide. Because no matter how many times you've claimed me as your own personal hero, you've never needed me to protect you. You're your own hero."

Her shoulders relaxed away from her ears.

"You always seem to know what to say to make me feel better." Setting her forehead against his chest, Camille stepped back but remained in the circle of his arms. Strong, creative, so passionate and alive. "That's why…that's why I've fallen in love with you."

Finn flinched.

Time stretched into a gut-wrenching, distorted fluid. He let his arms fall from around her and took a step back. The rational, distanced part of his brain took a back seat to the rush of terror forging a new neural pathway front and center, and panic tightened like a noose around his neck. Words died in his throat as a cold, dark dread unfurled in his chest. "You don't mean that."

Her bottom lip parted on a strong exhale. A humorless laugh bubbled up her bruised throat but was nothing like the sound he'd memorized before. "You said it yourself. I've survived what no one else has, Finn. I think that gives me a certain sense of self-awareness when it comes to this connection between us, and I think you feel it, too."

No. This was a routine assignment from Chief Deputy Remington Barton. He was the marshal assigned to protect this witness until her attacker's trial date. Nothing more. He didn't have feelings for her, didn't love her. Because that meant the admiration he felt for her over the past few days was more than a stress-induced consequence of adrenaline and danger, as he'd convinced himself when they'd fallen into bed together. They'd survived a killer determined to do whatever it took to prove himself to a veteran psychopath, and they'd both desperately needed that release. That was all. That didn't mean there was anything more than mutual attraction. Didn't mean there was a real connection between them outside of this investigation. Once the Carver was back behind bars, she'd move on with her life, and Finn would move on with his. Just as he had with every other witness he'd been assigned to protect. "I think it's best if I ask my chief deputy to reassign me from your protection detail."

He didn't love Camille. Couldn't. He'd lost the only person he'd ever cared about—loved—at the age of ten, and he'd sworn then he'd never feel that loss and that emptiness again. The hole left behind once they were gone wasn't worth the risk. And neither was she. Camille had her own life, a career she would want to get back to once this investigation was over. He'd still be here chasing fugitives, protecting other witnesses, and he didn't intend to stop. That left him only one option.

"What?" Camille lifted her uninjured hand toward her damaged shoulder as though attempting to keep herself upright, but the liquid exhaustion pooling in her aquamarine gaze gave away the effort. Jutting her chin out slightly, she stood her ground. "So I tell you I'm falling in love with you, and you say you want to be reassigned from my case? Why?"

"I can't be the one to protect you anymore. I have a check-in scheduled with Jonah Watson in fifteen minutes to go over the medical examiner's findings on Dr. Gruner's remains. I'm going to ask him to take over this detail." Finn brushed the back of his hand under his nose as a distraction from the watery gleam filling her eyes. He reached for his duffel bag, packed with his gear, clothing and sleeping bag. "Watson's a good marshal. He's a former bomb-disposal technician for the FBI, and he'll have a better perspective on this assignment than I do." He hauled his duffel bag strap over his shoulder, locking his jaw against the pain in his side from the stab wound, and headed for the safe house door. "He'll keep you safe. I promise."

The hollowness that'd set in a few days after his mother had been shot right in front of him expanded to the point that he couldn't take his next breath. His rib cage felt too tight, his heart threatening to beat straight out of his chest. He had to keep walking. Had to get to the door. He couldn't lose her, and damn it, if he let his emotions get in the way of his job, that was exactly what would happen. Anyone he'd ever cared about had been taken from him. His mom, his grandparents, the men and women he'd worked beside in Afghanistan. He couldn't let her become one more name on a long list of people who'd been ripped from his life. Walking away from her now might make him a coward, but he couldn't take that pain, the loneliness of losing one more person he cared about. Not again.

"I've heard a lot of promises over the past year, Marshal Reed," she said. "From a lot of different people."

Marshal Reed. Not Finn. He slowed, the agony of that small change splitting the dark cavern behind his sternum wider.

"From Jeff Burnes before he attacked me, from the police who found me covered in my own blood in that apartment, from the FBI agents promising me there was no way the Carver could find me once I was put in witness protection. Am I supposed to take your word for it that this new marshal will keep me safe, too?" Her voice carried across the safe house, echoing down the hallway. "You promised me we were going to do this together, but you're the one walking out the door right now. Don't I deserve to know why?"

The sooner he cut ties, the easier this would be on them both, and there was only one way to end this, to make her see the truth.

"You've pushed for this connection to be there between us from the beginning, Camille, but like I told you, I'm the marshal assigned to protect you. Nothing more. We're not friends. It's not my job to know what to say to make you feel better, and I don't have to explain myself. I was tasked to keep you alive, and I think it's better for both of us if I move off this detail. Before you misinterpret anything else." Tension knotted between his shoulder blades as the lie slipped from his mouth easily enough. He stared at the front door, his hand clamped around the duffel bag strap.

"And sleeping with me?" she asked. "Was that always part of your plan before you passed me off to some other marshal and ensured you'd never have to see me again, or did you just want to test how long I'd let you take advantage of me?"

His stomach rippled with sickness. He twisted his head over his shoulder but couldn't face her fully. "Arm the alarm after I'm gone. Don't open this door for anyone unless they knock twice."

"You made me believe I was important to you," she said. "Now I know it was all a lie."

Finn forced one foot in front of the other, wrenched the door open harder than needed and closed it behind him without looking back. If she'd still had any fantasies about him being some kind of hero, he'd finally succeeded in convincing her otherwise.

No. HE DIDN'T just get to walk away. He didn't get to push her off onto another marshal after everything they'd been through together. She couldn't think, couldn't breathe.

Camille clawed at the collar of her shirt for something to hold on to, grazing the edges of tape and gauze covering the gouges carved into her chest. She stared at the door. Waiting. He couldn't leave her here. She couldn't lose the only person she trusted. The walls suddenly seemed as if they were closing in, and there was nowhere for her to escape. She couldn't leave the safe house. Not with a killer masterminding every twist of this investigation. It didn't matter how much she wanted to follow him, to demand answers—she wouldn't put her life at risk. Marching toward the front door, she hit the arm button on the alarm as he'd instructed. Tears burned in her eyes as defeat swirled hot and angry in her chest.

Finn had promised her he wouldn't leave. What had changed?

Well, he'd given her an answer, hadn't he? Through the pounding of blood behind her ears, he'd told her exactly why nothing could ever happen between them beyond the conclusion of the investigation, and she hadn't listened.

You've pushed for this connection to be there between us from the beginning, Camille... Suffocating heaviness settled on her damaged shoulder and under her bruised, bloodied fingers. He was right. She'd done this. She'd put him in an impossible position nobody could live up to, but that didn't make her any less deserving of wanting to feel significant, to feel loved. Important. She'd prodded at his boundaries in an effort to latch onto something—someone—real and warm and reassuring, to make up for the past, but she'd pushed too hard. Until the only escape he'd seen had been to leave altogether. She'd just been so... starved for genuine human interaction, for someone to laugh with, someone who'd support her rather than ruin her, and Finn fit the shape of the invisible hole the Carver had created when he'd stolen her life perfectly.

Nausea washed into her stomach and spread to the far corners of her body. She didn't know how long she'd been standing there, watching the door, counting her inhales and exhales for the off chance the marshal she'd come to rely on would walk back into the safe house. She felt as though she was on a knife edge. The vulnerable, self-conscious woman she'd been since the attack in Chicago on one side, and the survivor Finn had convinced her she'd become on the other.

Had it really all been a lie?

Camille retraced her steps to her side of the bed and collected her camera from the nightstand. Instant calm buzzed in her veins with the added weight, despite the pull on her shoulder. Smoothing her thumb over the ridges in the lens cap, she closed her eyes. She couldn't do it. She couldn't be that woman who'd let her passion be ripped right from her hands, who'd broken because a man hadn't lived up to the promises that'd fallen from his lips. The woman who'd been overly aware of every look in her direction, listened for whispers spoken behind her back and looked for ulterior motives in the people around her.

But Finn's confidence in her, combined with his admiration, had made her feel stronger than all of that. Had made her believe that perfect fantasy version of herself could be more than a daydream, that she could be the woman she'd built up in her head.

She'd known this had been a possibility before falling into bed with him, that he wouldn't feel the same bond between them she'd felt since he'd taken the protection assignment, but that hadn't stopped her from taking the risk. She'd lived with a self-induced numbness for so long, even the possibility of heartbreak had drawn her to give in. But she'd been wrong about him, just as she'd been wrong about Jeff Burnes. Only unlike her former fiancé, Finn had tried to warn her. He'd never been the hero she'd defended him to be.

Camille moved her camera to her injured hand and threaded her fingers through her hair with the other. Her fantasy self wouldn't cry, wouldn't beg for him to stay, and neither would she. She switched the device on, the high-pitched whirl more comforting than ever before. She queued the last photo she'd taken, the one of him pretending to be asleep on the bed, and slid her thumb over the menu button to select Delete. He'd left to meet with the other marshal, who'd take over Finn's assignment as soon they were finished with their briefing, and there was nothing she could do about it. As long as the Carver was still out there, still waiting for trial, she'd be stuck here until Deputy US Marshal Watson said otherwise, but that didn't mean—

Something in the image caught her eye, a glare from Finn's nightstand she hadn't given much thought to until now. What was that? Bringing the cracked LCD monitor closer, she moved across the safe house until she'd positioned herself in the exact spot from where she'd taken the photo. She lifted her gaze beyond the camera, searching for the same glare, but it wasn't there. "That doesn't make sense."

She maneuvered between the bed and the wall and set her camera on the mattress. She pulled Finn's digital alarm clock to the edge of the nightstand. It was heavier than she'd imagined, and there was a second power cord crudely installed in the back. Why would a store-bought alarm clock need two power cords? One should've been enough. And even if the first cord had started malfunctioning, these types of clocks didn't cost much to replace. Why bother? Unless…

A thin needle of cold went through her. Camille rolled the shiny black clock in her hand. A section of the red digital numbers flickered wildly before becoming solid again, and she stilled. Gripping the entry point of the second power cord, she ripped the setup free.

And stared straight into a small reflective lens of a camera.

She dropped the clock, the plastic cracking as it hit the corner of the nightstand, and put as much space between her and the hidden surveillance device as she could. A terrible awareness slithered like a poison through her entire nervous system. Finn wouldn't have installed a hidden camera in his own safe house. He'd have no reason. Her gut instincts said he'd want less evidence of his witnesses under his protection. Not more. Which meant someone else had come inside. Someone else had installed the camera.

Had been watching them. Watching *her*.

Every second, every hour, every day since Finn had brought her here, they'd been surveilled without their knowledge. Her stomach soured. Even when they'd made love. Bile worked up her throat. She covered her mouth with the back of her hand as a weak distraction, but she wasn't sure anything could get rid of the emotional violation taking control. She had to focus. Turning her back to the nightstand, the small camera still in her hand, she scanned the rest of the safe house inch by inch. One camera wouldn't be enough to keep tabs on an intended target. There had to be others.

The weight of being watched made her dizzy, but she couldn't let it get to her. Not yet. As a photographer, she had to know the best angles to take the next shot and the one after that. The device in her hand didn't have a swivel feature. It'd been fixed in place inside the alarm clock and pointed directly toward the kitchen. If she needed to shoot the other side of the room, an angle in this camera's blind spot, she'd need a device positioned in that direction. Camille tilted back her head and centered on a possible source.

The small green light beside the smoke detector's test button had gone dark. Swallowing the tightness in her throat, she crossed to the kitchen counter and dragged a bar stool directly underneath the appliance. She climbed onto the stool, using the wall for balance, and twisted off the detector lid. Her hands quivered. The dark pinhole for the LED light wasn't a light at all but was another camera nearly invisible to the naked eye.

Two cameras. There were a million possibilities as to why they were here and who could've gotten access inside the safe house to install them.

She detached the power from the second device, presumably cutting off all recording, but not even severing the connection eased the tension building inside. "Finn."

She had to tell him. Marshals made enemies throughout their careers. There was a chance she hadn't been the target of this surveillance at all. Camille climbed down from the bar stool and tossed the hidden devices beside her camera on the bed. Working her injured arm into her coat, she slipped on her shoes and headed for the front door.

Two knocks echoed down the hallway before she'd made it more than a few steps.

She slowed. Finn's parting words rushed to the front of her mind. The marshal taking over her protective detail would knock twice. Jonah Watson would be able to contact Finn and tell him about the cameras. The US Marshals Service could use the devices to trace the feed back to the source and take it from there. She'd ask to be relocated to another district, and Finn's rejection would be behind her.

Camille punched in the six-digit code to disarm the security system. Hauling the heavy door open, she faced off with an all-too-familiar face she'd never thought she'd see again.

"Dr. Gruner." Only it wasn't him. Because according to the medical examiner who'd studied the remains Finn had recovered, the real Henry Gruner had been killed and left in the woods surrounding her house a year ago.

"Hello, Camille." Ear-length graying hair swooped down over a wrinkled forehead and the edge of the imposter's framed glasses. A large nose bubbled out toward full cheeks with a dusting of red across the bridge. Salt-and-pepper facial hair hid the outline of his mouth and most of his chin. He stepped over the threshold, hiking her pulse into overdrive. Upon first meeting this Dr. Gruner, she'd estimated his age to be around sixty, maybe sixty-five, what with the limp in his right leg, an old injury he'd claimed had been the reason he'd been medically discharged from the navy, but now the man closing in on her moved like a much younger version of himself.

The limp had disappeared. He stood tall, removing his glasses as she backed into the protective depths of the safe house. He let his glasses hit the floor and tugged at the edges of his mustache. Some kind of facial prosthesis peeled away from his nose before a gray wig slid from his scalp, revealing the killer she'd been running from for over a year.

Jeff Burnes.

The Carver.

He locked steel-gray eyes on her as her heel caught on the bar stool she'd left in the middle of the floor. "Did you get my anniversary present?"

Chapter Thirteen

"Illinois marshals got their fugitive about an hour ago." Deputy US Marshal Jonah Watson tapped Finn on the chest with the corner of a manila file folder. Iridescent blue eyes gleamed in clouded gray sunlight. The former FBI ordnance technician crossed his arms over his massive chest, cording muscle along his arms and neck. At two inches taller than Finn, Jonah had worked as a unit chief for the FBI's hazardous devices school as an instructor to support state and local bomb technicians before coming to serve as a deputy for the USMS. He'd worked for two years in Afghanistan for the bureau to analyze, investigate and re-create improvised explosive devices. His training made it nearly impossible for any detail to slip past the marshal's notice, and Finn needed his help with this case more than ever. "Bastard nearly made it across state lines. He was good. He's been laying low for the past week in an abandoned church as one of the homeless who sometimes stake out there at night, but someone noticed. Called in an anonymous tip right before he ran."

"That doesn't make sense." The Carver had escaped federal custody only to hang around Chicago for the past week? Finn took the file, his mind immediately jumping at the opportunity to focus on something other than the woman he'd left behind in the safe house. The pressure behind his rib cage still hadn't lifted, but Camille was safe. That was all that mattered. He'd done his job in keeping her alive, but now that honor had to go to another marshal. One who wouldn't make a mistake because he cared about the witness he'd been assigned to protect more than he wanted to admit.

Throughout this entire investigation she'd stood as a beacon of strength and the epitome of everything he'd feared since he'd been ten years old. The past several days had physically and emotionally drained him more than any other assignment, and it had everything to do with her, the most brilliant, honest and passionate creature he'd never seen coming. Whatever this connection she'd forged between them was, it wasn't simple. It didn't just require minimal effort, as he'd grown used to in his relationships with his fellow marshals, former combat buddies and the women he'd hooked up with. Camille came with a long history of trauma, healing and emotional neediness, and he had no idea how to support her in that or help her through it. She deserved someone who could open up the way she needed, someone she could trust, have fun with and be there when the nightmares surfaced. Not him.

Finn flipped through the file, trailing his finger down the report Illinois marshals had sent, then moved on to the photos. Every detail—no matter how small, how out of place—would get them one step closer to finding who had stalked Camille all the way to Oregon. He studied the first photo, a mug shot of a man he'd never seen before, and raised his gaze to Watson. Narrow jawline, short black hair with thick matching eyebrows, dark circles and a permanent exhaustion settling under brown eyes. "This isn't Jeff Burnes."

"It's kind of a good-news, bad-news situation." Watson tapped the face of the subject in the mug shot. "The guy they scooped up was wearing Burnes's prison uniform, but once they had their suspect in custody, they realized his face had been made to look like Burnes's with a bunch of makeup and silicone. The fugitive was wearing color-changing contacts and a wig to convince marshals they had their man. This guy? You're looking at Special Agent David Ronaldson of the FBI."

He recognized the name, and the world threatened to tilt on its axis. Finn had done his homework, right down to memorizing the law-enforcement officers and agents who'd worked Camille's case back in Chicago. Now Watson wanted him to believe David Ronaldson had been posing as Jeff Burnes all this time while in federal custody? What the hell was going on here? "Let me get this straight. You're telling me one of the agents assigned to find the Carver has been behind bars for a year disguised as his target? And nobody—not the FBI, not the prison warden, not the guards or Chicago PD—noticed until the man escaped?"

"This is what he looked like before." Watson peeled the mug shot away from the rest of the file, exposing the photo behind it, and Finn pinched the file cardstock harder. The man from the mug shot had been expertly transformed into someone else entirely. Not a trace of black hair, that narrow jawline or those light brown eyes. In his place, Finn could've sworn he was staring at a photo of the Carver if it hadn't been for the hundreds of hours he'd spent studying this case from the beginning until now. "Someone went through a lot of trouble to make sure the real Jeff Burnes wasn't behind bars. Enough trouble one of the agents assigned to the case stepped up as a body double. Agent Ronaldson still isn't talking without his lawyer present, which is going to be a couple more hours at least, but I have to think the Carver—the real Jeff Burnes—is the puppet master here."

Hell, if he hadn't seen the "after" photo, he never would've believed the "before." Outlines of leaves cut through the reflection off the photo paper, and every cell in Finn's body stilled. Agent Ronaldson had used makeup and a facial prosthesis to make himself look like the Carver, which meant Jeff Burnes was still out there, still looking for the one victim who'd gotten away. "Camille."

Finn dropped the file and sprinted as fast as he could back toward the safe house. Heavy footsteps fell in line behind him. He didn't have to explain the situation to Watson. He was already calling in for backup to their location. He just hoped to hell they'd make it in time. Pain radiated through his side and the balls of his feet as he rounded into the small alley leading to the safe house. Nearly ripping the handrail off the stairs, he charged toward the open front door. Camille wouldn't have left the safety of the remodeled garage, let alone left the front door open on her way out. The bastard had already been here. "No. No, no, no, no. Camille!"

The metal stairs shook under the fury of Watson's approach behind him.

Unholstering his weapon, Finn kicked the door wide and immediately cleared the hallway. He moved deeper, Watson taking point at his back. One of the kitchen bar stools had been pulled to the middle of the room. He motioned his colleague toward the bathroom with two fingers. The kitchen looked exactly as he'd left it. Smears of brownie mix stained the countertop and the sheets he hadn't gotten the chance to change before he'd left. The sink was filled with the evidence of his and Camille's extracurricular activities.

To the untrained eye, it might look like he and his witness had decided to bake brownies, then gone on with their day, but Watson had been trained to rely on the smallest details when it came to military ordnance, hand grenades, pipe bombs and any other kind of explosive device. The marshal's life had depended on it. There was no way Finn could explain his way out of this. The former FBI unit chief now knew Finn had had an intimate relationship with his witness. "Clear."

Finn lowered his weapon and studied the room again. He'd left Camille vulnerable for attack, but how had the Carver known she was here? How had he gotten past the alarm system in the first place or known Finn had left? No sign of a struggle, but his gut said Camille hadn't walked out of the safe house on her own. She wouldn't have taken the risk. He focused on the bare surface of the nightstand on her side of the bed, then her overnight bag on the floor. "Her camera is missing, but all of her other belongings are still in the duffel bag you packed. If she'd walked out that door on her own, she would've taken everything."

"The smoke detector has been disassembled, as

well as the alarm clock I assume sat on this night-stand. There are pieces of it all over the floor." Watson holstered his sidearm and dove into his coat pocket for a pair of gloves. Latex snapped against his wrists, then he picked up the fragments and arranged them on the nightstand. This was what Watson did, what he'd been trained to do during his time in the FBI. He'd analyze the pieces of the puzzle scattered over any given landscape and spend a grueling amount of time re-creating the original device and determining how it functioned. "There are two power sources here. One for the alarm clock, and one for something else. A hidden camera maybe."

"Damn it." Finn studied the bar stool left in the middle of the small space, then shifted his attention to the smoke detector. "That's not the same detector I installed when I remodeled this place. It's been replaced."

"Most likely with another camera." Watson moved beside Finn. "Someone was watching you here. Watching her. They knew the location of your safe house and infiltrated it without you knowing."

"And then they came in here and took her and the cameras." Uselessness filled him, suffocating any hope he'd had of finding a lead on Camille's location. "How? The only people I told about this place were you and Remi." Understanding hit, and his gut pitched hard. "And she would've made a note in Camille's file in the Warrant Information Network."

"The marshal in Chicago. The autopsy showed the victim had been killed two hours before her log-in information had been used by Miles Darien to find out where Camille had been relocated. Illinois marshals should've disabled access after the ME's findings were released," Watson said. "But there's a chance it was overlooked. Whoever took her might still have access to the system, and maybe any security protocols you've put in place for your witness."

"I told Camille not to open the door for anyone unless they knocked twice. She gave her abductor access without knowing who was on the other side because the bastard followed the protocol noted in her WIN file." This was on him. He'd left her unprotected, turned his back on her and everything she'd needed from him because he'd been too afraid to confront his own damn weaknesses. But he wouldn't fail her again. "It's the Carver. This whole investigation is centered around him. The attack last year, her relocating to Florence, Miles Darien getting access to her location, Agent Ronaldson's escape from federal custody. It's all been planned from the beginning, a manipulation to throw us off. This is personal for him. Camille is the only victim who got away, and he's going to make sure it doesn't happen again, but he couldn't have gone far."

"Twenty minutes gives him a good head start, though." Watson discarded his gloves as screeching tires and echoed voices sounded down the hall. Backup had arrived.

Finn extracted his phone from his pocket and punched in the web address for *Global Geographic*, then scrolled through the archive of articles he'd studied over the past few days. "Jeff Burnes was a writer for *Global Geographic*. He and Camille only worked on a handful of assignments together, but there's one location within driving distance." He found the article he'd been looking for and jammed the phone into Watson's hands as he headed for the door. "He's taking her here."

Something squished under his boot, and Finn froze. Lifting his foot, he studied the skin-colored shape that'd been discarded up against the wall. He hadn't seen it before now, had been focused on clearing the scene and finding Camille, but now he understood. Silicone shaped to look like a human nose. Her abductor had either removed the appearance-changing prosthetic, or Camille had fought back and torn it away from her attacker's face. Either way, Finn was certain now.

The man who'd hurt her had come to finish the job.

COLD WATER SPLASHED against her face, ripping her from unconsciousness. The ground was soft, gritty, and shifted under the weight of her shoulder as Ca-

mille turned onto her back. Her head fell to the opposite side. Sand stuck to the back of her neck, her
hands, her hair. Gray clouds changed shapes over a
long, unoccupied stretch of beach, divots of one set
of footprints leading toward her. Blurred trees and
black rocks went in and out of focus, her arms and
legs somehow heavier aside from the added weight
of her soaked clothing.

What…?

"I remember the first time I saw you with this camera. It was on our very first assignment for *Global
Geographic* together. You'd been assigned as my photographer for an article I was writing, and I remember
thinking I'd finally found my equal," he said.

That voice. Every nerve ending she owned screamed
warning as the haze of whatever sedative he'd injected
her with clung to her senses. The familiar click of her
camera reached her ears over the noise-canceling swell
of ocean waves. He was close, closer than she'd realized, and a fist of dread knotted in her gut.

Sand gritted under heavy footsteps. "You were the
most beautiful woman I'd ever seen—intelligent,
creative, passionate."

Recognition flared as she took in the stretch of
damp beach, the bright red-and-white lighthouse positioned on the cliffs that'd served as a beacon of
hope and relief to lost sailors for more than a cen-
tury and the never-ending dark expanse of ocean on

her left. She'd been here before. On assignment for *Global Geographic*. It'd been a couple of years, but she hadn't forgotten. The beach stretched for nearly a quarter of a mile in each direction, a thick line of trees stood guard at her back and the choppy waves sliding toward her wouldn't do her a damn bit of good.

No matter which direction she ran, the Carver would catch her.

A humorless laugh broke through the ringing in her ears as she turned over onto her stomach. And there he was. A sharp jawline contrasted the roundness of the man he'd posed as for the last year. His medium brown hair had been parted slightly to the right, giving him more of a boyish appearance, rather than looking like the manipulative killer she'd known him to be. He was handsome, distinguished, with an easy smile and gray eyes that'd once promised to give her the world. He towered over her at six foot one, her camera in his hand. "I'd never met anyone with half as much passion for their work as you, and that's when I knew I had to have you. That together, we would make the ultimate team. At least until the moment you let that marshal touch you."

Ultimate team for what? Camille dug her fingers into the sand, her shoulder protesting the paralysis of desperation to escape. "How...? The marshals said you escaped prison a week ago, but you've been posing as my therapist for a year."

"I'll have to admit, that was a stroke of genius I wasn't sure would play out as I'd planned." Jeff raised his eye to her camera's viewfinder and snapped a photo of her. The flash blinded her for a split second before color returned. He lowered the device, crouching beside her. Sand clung to his slacks and black shoes. "I've always been very good at reading people, Camille, figuring out what they wanted. Within seconds of approaching my target, I'd know exactly what their greatest desires were, what they feared. In every instance I narrowed my focus on my next victim, I had the power to grant them everything they wanted or ruin their life beyond repair." His gaze lifted from her, out to sea, brighter than she remembered, and a deep muscular quake shook through her. This wasn't her former fiancé standing over her. This was a killer in his element. The Carver. "It just so happened, I discovered that same talent could be used to find people with…similar interests. Like one of the FBI agents assigned to investigate the six women who'd been found strangled with the word *mine* carved into their chests throughout Chicago."

Surprise coiled through her. "What?"

"Believe me, I know how it sounds, but I couldn't pass up the opportunity to see how far I could push a man who'd taken an oath to protect the innocent. Once I realized his obsessive interest to find me lay in the inner workings of how and why I killed my victims and not some warped sense of duty the bureau brainwashed their agents to believe in, it wasn't hard to convince him he could lose everything. I had the power to take his career, his family, everything. Unless he did exactly as I told him. Over several months, I was able to pinpoint and use his own fear against him, mold him into the perfect body double." Straightening, Jeff centered those steel-gray eyes on her, and the muscles down her spine spasmed in warning. "As you've already seen, I'm quite good at blending in. Stood to reason I could also make Agent Ronaldson resemble my likeness. At least, enough that the FBI didn't know they had one of their own in cuffs instead of the Carver. I was arrested that night in Chicago after surgeons pieced me back together from your knife, but he was the one who ensured I never set foot behind bars."

"And he went along with it because you'd threatened to expose him for what he really was." There was another piece of the puzzle still out there, one Jeff Burnes had recruited solely to convince the FBI Jeff Burnes was the man behind bars. "Miles Darien was right. You killed Jodie Adler. You left her in the woods behind my house, knowing the marshals service would find her and I'd connect the location to the photograph you encouraged me to take that day. And your protégé? Was Miles Darien another stray you blackmailed to do your bidding or was he just a fan of your work?"

Jeff circled into her vision, his attention on the camera in his hands. "Miles played his part well, until he betrayed my trust by coming after you. I'm obviously disappointed to lose someone of such talent, but if your marshal hadn't killed Miles, I would have. I gave him specific instructions he was never to lay a hand on you, and he broke the rules."

"Why?" The way he talked of murder, so casually, as though a human life meant nothing more than crushing an ant under his heel, hollowed her from the inside. How could she not have seen him for what he was? How could she have let him into her home, into her bed, into her life without knowing something was wrong? Camille clawed at the sand, mentally gauging how fast she could run for the trees or the cliffs with a small amount of sedative still pulling at her arms and legs. Tourist season had slowed months ago. Losing him in the woods would be her best chance at survival. At least long enough until night fell, and she could run without being seen. A shiver chased across her shoulders as her body temperature dropped. Another spray of seawater added to the cold settling into her bones. Bitterness entered her voice. "Why do all of this? Why pose as a therapist pretending to help me? Why lie about a break-in to Dr. Gruner's office and make me choose Jodie Adler's final resting place? Why install surveillance equipment in the safe house? Is all of this just so you could finish killing me yourself?"

"I told you, Camille. When I choose my target, I have the power to give them everything they want or the power to destroy them. I didn't want to kill you. I realized I'd made a mistake last Valentine's Day when I set out to add you to my collection of victims, right around the moment you stabbed me with your steak knife. For the first time I could remember, I'd been driven by a sudden desperation to hide what I was from you. Something I'd never done with any of my other victims. You were sitting across the kitchen table from me, so perfect, so enticing, and all I could think was that if you knew the truth about me, it was only a matter of time before you left. I obsessed over that idea all throughout the day and when dinner came, I attacked, only…you changed everything. I had my hands around your throat, that brightness I'd come to admire was slipping from your eyes, and right then I felt…empty. Like I was killing a piece of myself." He tossed her camera into the sand, cloud-shaded sunlight revealing the photo he'd queued on the LCD monitor. One she'd taken of Finn.

He reached for her, pinching her chin between his thumb and index finger when she pulled away, and forced her to look him straight in the eye. Tearing at the collar of her shirt, he exposed the tape and gauze covering the gouges on her chest. Stinging pain seared across her nerve endings as he ripped the dressing from her skin. "I meant what I said when I started carving those letters into your chest, Camille. You're mine. Not Miles's. Not the marshal's. Mine. We were so much alike, you and me. We both had so much passion for what we did. I was ready to give you everything. Then you let a man who left you unprotected and alone try to take what's mine. Now, you're nothing more than an insignificant part of my past and the past of your marshal, and no one is coming to save you this time."

Truth resonated through her, but Finn had been right about one thing.

She'd survived that past because she'd become her own hero.

"You're sick. I don't know how I wasn't able to see that before, but I will spend the rest of my life making sure you pay for what you've done." Camille wrenched out of his hold, fisted a handful of sand and threw it directly into his eyes. She shot to her feet, fighting every last bit of the sedative he'd given her, and sprinted across the beach. Wet hair whipped around her face as she ran, but she didn't dare focus on anything more than making it to the trees. Just a little farther. She pumped her legs as hard as she could, her muscles protesting the extra effort. Her wet clothing chafed at her skin, but she couldn't slow down. Couldn't look back.

Ten feet to the tree line. Five.

A hardened wall of muscle tackled her from behind.

The beach distorted in her vision as she slammed face-first into the ground. Sand and debris clung to her face and neck as the heaviness on her back disappeared and a strong grip flipped her over. She kicked out but missed. Camille shoved to her feet. She couldn't see anything with the grit in her eyes. Defeat hooked into her and wouldn't let go, but it didn't stop her from swinging her fist out in one last desperate attempt to escape. "Why are you doing this?"

"It's quite a rush, you know, having all the power to lift someone beyond their wildest fantasies or to tear them down to nothing. I'm going to destroy you, Camille." Pain seared across her skull as he yanked her into his chest by the hair at the back of her head. A jolt of movement tugged her down before a mechanical crunching filled her ears. Her camera. Her comfort zone, her lifeline… He'd destroyed it, and the loss speared straight through her heart. He spun her to face him, that familiar spice of cologne sticking in her nose and throat, and ground the sand stuck to her face into her skin with his fingers. "You did me a favor all those months ago. Your passion for photography showed me a singular focus was the only way to truly be happy. Now I'm going to do the same for you."

Chapter Fourteen

The Carver had become Dr. Henry Gruner.

Finn wasn't sure how, other than by the use of silicon prosthetics, some makeup and possible changes in his voice. The bastard had sat across from Camille in that office for hours during their appointments. And she'd never known. Camille had been right all along. Jeff Burnes could become whatever his victims—whatever law enforcement—needed him to be. What he wanted them to believe. The Carver had posed as her therapist to study his victims, torment them, direct them to do what he wanted, all in the name of helping her heal.

Finn pressed the SUV's accelerator into the floor. The growl of the engine vibrated through him as he pushed the vehicle around the next curve of the highway. Blood beat a terrible rhythm behind his ears every moment Camille was out there with that psychopath. Damn it. He should've been there. He should've known someone had been watching her.

Not just someone. The Carver.

The very nightmare she'd been running from for a year. He'd promised to protect her, but with one crack in his defenses against recognizing he'd felt more for her than he had anyone else, he'd run. He'd left her to face her fears alone in order to protect himself from his own but instead put himself in a position to lose everything.

He'd gone out of his way over the past twenty-five years to avoid having to feel the pain and anguish that came with losing someone he loved, to avoid having to face the fact he wasn't strong enough or capable enough to protect who he cared about. But right now, the force driving him to get to her as fast as possible wasn't born of duty to protect his witness. It was something deeper, something he'd tried to deny since he'd taken down Miles Darien seconds before the bastard had another chance to hurt her, but Finn couldn't ignore it any longer. The thought of anything happening to Camille overrode his own sense of self-preservation. Because despite all the barriers he'd built between them, he'd fallen in love with her, too.

There wasn't anything that would stop him from getting to her.

She'd given him strength to pull himself up that hill after Miles Darien had stabbed him. She'd shown him the perfect example of survival and emotional honesty he'd needed all these years. She'd bulldozed everything he'd believed about vulnerability, weakness and the effects of trauma and somehow defied the very concept of victim. Camille Goodman was… She was everything, and he'd spend the rest of his life proving she was the most important part of his life if that was what she required.

A long line of marshal vehicles and police cruisers tried to keep up behind him, sirens and patrol lights flashing bright in the descending dusk. The entire Florence Police Department and the Oregon district office of the United States Marshals Service had responded to Watson's call for backup and followed Finn in a race to recover his witness. "I'm coming for you, Red. I'm going to find you. Just hold on a little while longer."

Jeff Burnes reveled in his work and what he was: a killer. It was unlikely the bastard had limited himself to only killing Jodie Adler during his time here in Florence, but no other bodies had been discovered in or around the area over the last year. The Carver had either become expertly practiced in disposing of and hiding his bodies, or he'd wanted Jodie Adler to be found in those woods. To announce his presence to the authorities, to Camille.

Heceta Beach stretched out on either side as he twisted his SUV toward the beach's nearest access point. The point of the cliffs took the brunt of high winds and violent waves, but they wouldn't be enough in the oncoming storm. Dark clouds blacked out the sun in a rolling flood, and the hairs on the back of Finn's neck stood on end. After throwing the vehicle in Park, he got out and rounded the bumper. He lifted the tailgate over his head. Cold worked under his clothing as he tugged the duffel bag Chief Deputy Remington Barton asked every deputy under her supervision to carry. He pulled his Kevlar vest, extra ammunition and his backup weapon from his supplies. Screeching tires and sirens died as the rest of the team filled the parking lot.

Remington Barton—Remi to the marshals under her command—shouted orders to the Florence officers as they climbed from their vehicles. With long black hair, authority coating her orders and a lean, muscular frame ready to take on any threat, the chief deputy had taken absolute control of the scene. "Listen up! I want roadblocks at every access point to this beach and a perimeter out to half a mile. Nobody comes into or leaves this area without my saying so, do you understand?" She pulled a photo from her vest and held it up with one hand, her weapon in the other. "Jeff Burnes—also known as the Carver—is highly dangerous, presumably armed and very adept at disguising himself. He will kill you if it gives him the opportunity to escape so keep your heads in the game. Florence PD will set the perimeter while marshals search every inch of this beach, the light-house and cliffside. We're not leaving here until we find Jeff Burnes and his current hostage, Camille Goodman. No matter how long it takes." She nodded. "Stay in teams. Stay safe."

The Florence PD officers scattered, echoing orders among themselves.

Deputy US Marshal Dylan Cove, a recent transfer into their district due to Beckett Foster's absence, unholstered his weapon from the shoulder holster beneath his windbreaker and checked his weapon. The former private investigator hid behind unmanaged beard growth and wild dark hair. Almost as though he'd just rolled out of bed. He didn't look like much, but Finn had done his research on the newest addition to their office. From what he'd been able to piece together, Cove and the chief deputy had crossed paths more than once before Remi had left the small-town police force back in New Jersey. If his boss trusted Dylan Cove as a marshal, then so did Finn. The investigator had rough edges, secrets, but all that mattered was he was one more set of eyes in the search for Camille with miles of beach on either side of them. "What makes you think your fugitive chose this spot to finish his work?"

"It means something to him and Camille. This was the location of one of their first assignments for *Global Geographic* and within driving distance of

the safe house. I've studied every homicide attrib-
uted to this guy. He doesn't just choose his victims
then kill them out of some inner drive he can't control. He studies them, gets to know their habits, gains
their trust in order to destroy their identities. He's the
most dangerous kind of killer. He's a snake, one who
can control himself and wait as long as he needs to
before the moment is right." And Camille's moment
had come. But Finn wouldn't rush onto that beach
as he had the woods around her house. He wasn't
going to let her abductor get the best of him this time.
Jeff Burnes might've gathered as much intel on his
victims as he had access to, but Finn had the entire
USMS behind him and a year's worth of research
invested in this hunt. "He's gone out of his way to
study her for the past year, to pose as someone she
trusted in order to get access to her most personal
details and cause the most damage. She isn't just the
one who got away. She's the only one who got away.
He brought her here to prove this is as personal for
her as it is for him, and he'll do everything in his
power to make her feel isolated, alone and scared.
We're going to prove him wrong."

Jonah Watson took position at Finn's right and
handed out radios. "We split up into teams. Remi and
Cove head south. Finn and I will head north. Stay in
contact. No one's a hero on their own."

Heroes aren't given their status because they pre-

*vent the bad things from happening. It's because they
will do anything to stand up to the people responsible, and that's what you've done for me.*

A hero. The word stuck in Finn's brain as he attached the radio to his vest and headed for the beach.
The crush of angry waves drowned the ringing in
his ears as Watson followed up behind him. Camille
had called him her hero. He'd hated the label, and yet
nothing would stop him from doing the right thing
by her, to bring her home and take down the killer
who'd targeted her. He wasn't a hero. Not in the general sense of his job as a US marshal like Karen Reed
had been, but he'd take the title for Camille now. He'd
stand up to the Carver for her. He'd make sure her
attacker never hurt her or anyone else again.

He and Watson jogged along the outer edge of the
beach. The storm picked up pace as though mirror-
ing the panicked and rage-fueled war waging inside
his chest. The sand threatened to suck him down and
hold him back, but he pushed through the pain in
his side and the cold seeping past skin and muscle.
Thousands of divots marked the beach as the wind
picked up and the waves reached farther up the shore.
In seconds, half of them had been wiped away, but
one divot in particular drew him closer as the tide
climbed higher. A dark patch of sand pulled his attention from the outskirts of the beach, and Finn
jogged to investigate.

Not sand. A camera.

Where was she? He shouted back to Watson, "She was here!"

"Then they couldn't have gotten far." Watson's voice was whipped away on another gust of wind.

Finn turned to face off with the cliffs reaching high overhead that protected the Heceta Head Lighthouse from the onslaught of the storm. In every case file he'd studied of the Carver's work, the killer had brought his victim somewhere private. The flat plateaus were too exposed here. Jeff Burnes wouldn't take the risk of being spotted by tourists, the lighthouse keeper or guests of the inn on the same slope. He'd want to have Camille all to himself but still have the chance of getting away with her murder when her body was discovered. Rain spit against the side of his face in painful pricks, and Finn turned to the marshal behind him. "The assignment Camille and Jeff Burnes were on here. None of the photos were of the lighthouse."

Understanding contorted Watson's expression as he lowered his gaze from the cliffs to a collection of small islands at the point of the mountain. "They were of the caves under the lighthouse."

And the tide was coming in.

THICK MOISTURE COATED the lining in her lungs.

Jeff's punishing grip dragged her over uneven,

rocky terrain, her breathing echoing back to her in the darkness. She didn't have to get the sand out of her eyes to know where he'd taken her. Her shoes squished with the ocean water captured in her socks, and another rush of ice water climbed up her legs. Her dropping body temperature was going to throw her into shock before the Carver ever got his chance to finish what he'd started last Valentine's Day. Her shoe caught on smooth rock, and Camille tripped forward.

Only there was no one to catch her when she hit the ground this time. Water flooded through the collar of her shirt and drenched her face and chest. The cave she and Jeff had been assigned to explore for *Global Geographic* absorbed her groan as she struggled to get to her feet. It'd taken several attempts battling with the ocean tide to get the shots she'd wanted for the article from inside the cave and one near-death experience to get out, and he'd brought her here to kill her. The receding wave tugged at her ankles as it escaped the mouth of the cave, taking the feeling in her toes and the bottoms of her feet with it.

"Whether you want to admit it or not, Camille, we're not so different after all. It's our chosen paths that separate us. Your passion for photography. My passion for hurting people. You were my muse, the example I looked up to when I found myself getting bored with the routine of every kill. I knew all I had to do was to get a little more creative, just as you kept pushing for the most difficult assignments with the magazine, and suddenly, the spark would reignite." Jeff's voice bounced off the walls all around her, vibrated through her. Became part of her. "We're two sides of the same coin, you and I, and when you left, when you ran from me, I found myself all over again. Only stronger. You were the first victim of mine to fight back, and the thrill of that truth, the thrill of the chase, was unlike anything I'd felt before."

His shadowed outline and the cave as a whole both darkened as the sun disappeared behind a veil of gray cloud cover, but the slim shape of a blade stood stark against the white backdrop of the entrance. "That's why I pushed you to take that photo after you came to Florence, Camille. You were lost for a while, but I knew if I pushed you, I could help you find yourself again. Just as you helped me."

He took a step toward her, but she couldn't counter. Not without going deeper into the cave, not without cutting off her path to escape. "All those other women, the ones who didn't escape, women like Jodie Adler and so many others I've come to enjoy since coming to Oregon. They were some of my best work. You thought you experienced hell that night at dinner? I can confidently tell you they suffered so much more. Because of you. You see, I don't need you anymore, Camille. You're just going to be another name on the Carver's belt when I'm finished with you."

"You talk too much." Numbness that had nothing to do with the lower temperatures spread through her. Fear took hold as the last of the waves retreated from the entrance to the cave. It was only a matter of time before the next one raced into the small space where the Carver had her trapped, and unless she found some way around him before the cave flooded, she'd die here.

The constant ticking of rain meeting the surface of the ocean kept in time with her heart rate. She clenched her fists at her sides. Flashes of that Valentine's Day dinner in their shared apartment played in slow motion across her mind. Jeff coming across the table, his hands so strong around her neck as he pinned her against the floor. The image changed to a masked Miles Darien closing in on her in the houseboat as she clutched nothing more than a piece of glass from a broken frame. In both instances, her attacker had been stronger, faster, more violent and desperate to claim her as their own, but she couldn't let him win. Not again.

Camille lunged, cocking back her uninjured arm and throwing a punch as hard as she could. He wasn't going to kill her. She wasn't a fighter, but she wasn't going to let him hurt anyone else. The man of her nightmares dodged to the right and turned back to wrap his hand around her wrist. Wrenching her into him, he pinned her in place before twisting her arm behind her back. Pressure built in her shoulder socket with sickening fury as Jeff forced her head down. She squeezed her eyes closed, tried to breathe through the pain, but he wouldn't let up. Blackness swept across her vision.

"I used to think you were special, Camille." The Carver pressed his mouth against her ear and hauled her back hard enough that her shoulder almost popped free of the socket. A chill swept across her collarbone as he placed his knife at her throat. "But you're just like the rest of them. Scared, weak, alone. And mine."

"She's not alone," a familiar voice said from behind. "And she sure as hell isn't yours, Burnes. Now let her go."

The cave and individual rocks under her feet blurred as Jeff spun her around to face off with two muscular outlines at the mouth of the cave. The blade bit into her skin, and she clutched at her attacker's wrists to keep the edge from sinking deeper. Sun pierced through the heavy cover of clouds, highlighting the marshal who'd requested to be reassigned from her case. Exhilaration and terror swept through her. No. He wasn't supposed to be here. He had to get out. Now. "Finn."

What was he doing here? How had he found her? Jeff increased the pressure around her throat, cutting off precious oxygen, and her warning for the marshals to get out of the cave before the next wave hit died in her chest.

"Jeff Burnes, it's over. You're not getting out of here without us. It's up to you whether you leave in cuffs or with a bullet in your head." Both Finn and the marshal he'd handed off her protection detail to shortened the distance between themselves and the Carver, with her positioned between them.

One pull of the trigger, one slice of the knife, and it'd all be over.

Gold dollars of sunlight bounced off the waves, sharpening the angles of Finn's bearded jawline, emphasizing the compelling blue eyes she'd stupidly come to trust. No matter what happened now, nothing would change between them. He'd made his feelings about her—about her need for emotional connection—clear. He'd tracked her and the Carver here for one reason: to do his job. "If you hurt her, there won't be anywhere for you to run. Nowhere you can hide from me. So why don't you make this easier on yourself and drop the knife before I put a bullet through you?"

"This is the man you trusted with your body after what I did to it? You know he doesn't care about you. You know you were just another witness he'd never see again once the case was closed. Who's to say how many others there have been?" Jeff smoothed a section of her soaked hair back behind her shoulder with his free hand, and a sudden burst of bile collected in her throat. "You were always special to me. The letters I carved into your chest are physical proof. You always will be mine."

His. Her fingers tingled with the same sensation as they had when she'd picked up her camera.

No matter how many times you've claimed me as your own personal hero, you've never needed me to protect you. You're your own hero. Finn's words wound through her, past the fear, past the uncertainty and straight into that spot she'd felt like a piece of her had been missing. He'd been right. As much as it hurt to think she'd never be anything more than the witness he'd been assigned to protect when this was finished, Finn had been right. Every time she'd been attacked—by Jeff, by Miles Darien, by the loss of her identity when she hadn't been able to go near her camera—she'd survived. She'd gotten back on her feet and faced off with the next setback, the next threat. She'd been her own damn hero. "I used to believe I was just another one of your victims, Jeff, but I know better now. I was never yours. I was never the Carver's or Miles's. I let what you did to me affect my confidence, who I was, but you were never able to claim me. I'm a survivor, and that is something you can never take from me."

Camille shot her elbow into her attacker's midsection as hard as she could. The knife slipped from her throat, and she spun, shoving him back with everything she had. His growl vibrated through her as the knife came down. She braced for the pain, hands shooting out in front of her to protect her face.

"No!" A hard push at the middle of her back sent her forward as two gunshots exploded from behind.

She landed on all fours on top of a row of smooth rocks leading out to sea. Pain pierced through the numbness already penetrating from her soaked clothing in her shoulder. Twisting her head back toward where she'd been mere seconds ago, she saw Jeff standing there. Absolutely still.

The rising roar of the ocean was the only warning she had before water gushed around her ankles, then rose up her calves and above her waist. She was out of time. They all were. Camille reached out to him at the same time Finn reached for her, but her fingers slipped, and suddenly he was gone beneath the surface of the wave. "Finn!"

The Carver lowered his chin to his chest, watched the darkening stains of red seep toward his waist as the water climbed his tall frame. The gunshots. He turned to face her, enough for her to realize he wasn't going to leave this cave alive after all. Just as Finn had warned. "You'll always be…mine."

The ocean dragged her under.

Chapter Fifteen

The current thrust him upward. Sharp pain exploded at the back of his head as the water shot him straight into the ceiling of the cave. Pressure built in his ears as seawater twisted him around until he wasn't sure which way was up. He frantically tried to grab on to something—anything—to get some kind of bearing, but there was only a black ocean of nothingness. Salt stung the wound at the back of his skull and soaked the bandage of the stab wound in his side. The pain said he was still alive, but he couldn't breathe. Couldn't see a damn thing in front of him.

Camille. Where was Camille?

He kicked and thrashed as bubbles tickled across his skin and through his clothing. She had to be here. He couldn't have lost her just as they'd been freed from the Carver's manipulative game.

This wasn't a killer holding a knife to her throat. This wasn't his own fear of opening himself up to love another person holding him back. This was out of his control, and it took everything inside him not to give in to the panic of losing her after what they'd been through the past several days.

His chest compressed, his lungs spasming for oxygen. He had to keep calm. The harder he fought against the wave, the faster he'd burn through his oxygen. Jeff Burnes had brought Camille here knowing that if he'd been successful in killing her, her body would've been swept out to sea. Maybe never to be seen again. But Finn wasn't going to let that happen. Not now. Not ever. He hadn't put two bullets in the bastard to let the Carver take her from him now.

Muted sunlight pierced through the water to his right, and his body jerked in the same direction. The water was receding. The current took the last ounces of his will for control out of the equation and pulled him toward the mouth of the cave. Jagged walls cut into the exposed skin of his arms as he ripped past, but just as he tried to clutch onto one piece in particular, a wall of red hair skimmed across his face.

Camille.

He shot out his hand, grabbing onto whatever he could reach and wrapped his forearm around her middle. Her fingers sank into the backs of his shoulders as they rocked and turned in the shallowing water until sunlight penetrated through the thick darkness. He encircled her in his arms, holding on to her as another wave slammed down on top of them. The force knocked them far beneath the ocean surface as churning waters blanketed them in a wall of white.

Then there was calm.

For the briefest of moments, the waters settled enough for him to get his bearings, kick off from the bottom and shoot them upward. They broke through the surface, both gasping for air and clinging to one another. The swells wouldn't let up, but Finn could still see the shoreline. They hadn't been spit out too far into the vast engulfing ocean. Forty, maybe fifty feet at most. Dizziness threatened to take control as his body battled to catch up with the shot of oxygen and pressure release. Intertwining his hand into hers, he kicked toward the shore. Vehicles dove down from the parking lot and streaked across the sand toward them, sirens and lights pulsing through the blanketing night. The Carver was dead. The investigation would be closed, and Camille was free of the threat that'd chased her for a year, but Finn wasn't ready to let her walk away. Not by a long shot. "We can make it. Just a little farther."

Another wave pushed them toward the beach until he felt his boots dragging in the soft sand. He hauled himself to his feet. Cold water and exhaustion tugged him back toward the vast expanse of blackness behind them, but he had to keep going. He had to make sure she was okay. They hit land. Hanging on to Camille at his side, he slid his hands over her arms in rapid lines to bring back some of the warmth to her skin as paramedics and his team converged on their position. He raised his voice over the crushing groan of the ocean at their backs. "Hang on, Red. We're almost there."

Two paramedics raced to them, one at his side, one at Camille's, and helped them from the last few inches of water. Tremors buried deep near his bones clenched his muscles so damn hard he could barely move.

A series of coughs pierced through the constant spitting of rain a few feet behind him. Jonah Watson dragged himself onto shore. "A little help would've been nice."

Remington Barton and Dylan Cove arrived with Mylar emergency blankets and tried to help them up the sloping beach to the parking lot, but he couldn't let go of his witness's hand. Not yet. "You have every reason not to talk to me after what I did, Red, but I need you to know. I didn't leave because you were pushing for a connection I didn't want between us. I left because I wanted it as much as you did, maybe even more."

Her teeth chattered, lines of water coursing down her face.

"You hurt me, Finn. More than Jeff Burnes or Miles Darien ever could." She wrenched her hand from his, his teammates backing off to give her room. "I can heal from a stab wound or from the letters carved into my chest, but you... What you did was so much worse. I trusted you with my secrets. I gave you something I've never been able to share with anyone else when we made love. You made me feel like I was important to you then walked away as if I was nothing."

"I know, and I'll have to live with that mistake for the rest of my life," he said. "The thought of someone ripping you away from me like they took my mom all those years ago... I was protecting myself, but when I realized you'd been taken, the thought of never knowing what this could be between us hurt far more than the past ever could. I love you, Red. You make me feel stronger when the whole world is collapsing around me and I don't see a way out. You're the reason I'm standing here at all after Miles Darien stabbed me, and I'll do whatever it takes to prove to you that without you, I'm nothing but that scared ten-year-old kid who lost his mom to a fugitive that night."

The hard creases between her eyebrows softened. "I need someone who isn't afraid to face the hard things with me, Finn. Someone who will be there when the nightmares come and is willing to try to understand what I'm going through. I need to know you're not going to leave me to face what comes next alone."

"I'm yours, Red." Water streaked into his eyes, but Finn didn't dare blink for fear she'd disappear from right in front of him all over again. "As long as you'll have me."

"You owe me chocolate." The words barely made it past blue lips and chattering teeth, and he couldn't help but laugh.

"I'll buy you as much chocolate as you want for the rest of your life." Sand clung to his boots and jeans as he stepped into her and lowered his mouth to hers. An explosion of heat destroyed the hollowness he'd held on to all these years but couldn't fight off the shivers quaking through them.

"Deal. Now get me out of here before we can't move." They hit the asphalt parking lot as one, and hell, if he had anything to say about it, they'd leave as one, too.

Two officers raced toward the beach with a stretcher between them, a long black bag draped over the top. The EMT next to Camille helped her step into the back of the ambulance. He didn't know how the body hadn't been washed out to sea, but Jeff Burnes was awaiting for someone to collect him from the sand. Finn could still feel the jolt of the gun in his hand when he'd pulled that trigger. He'd done what he'd had to in order to protect the person he cared about the most, and right then, he understood his mother had done the same all those years ago. Karen Reed hadn't thought about what would happen if she'd put herself in front of that bullet, just as Finn hadn't stopped to think about what would happen when he'd raised his weapon. He'd only followed his instincts. Followed his heart in order to protect what mattered to him the most. Camille.

"Marshal Reed?" the EMT at his side asked.

Finn leveraged his weight against the back of the ambulance and extended his arm out for the emergency tech to take his blood pressure.

"Tell me it's over." Camille set her temple against his shoulder, looking out over the black expanse of ocean that'd nearly taken them both. The Mylar space blanket covering her from neck to toes reflected the last few rays of dying sunlight.

"It's over." He swept her wet hair out of his beard and rested his chin on the crown of her head. "He can't hurt you anymore."

"He hurt so many others, women who are still out there." Her voice wavered, but whether it was from their dropping body temperatures or from processing everything that'd happened, he didn't know. Either way, he'd be there to help her carry the burden. "He told me Jodie Adler and the others he'd enjoyed since coming to Oregon had suffered so much more than I did. Because I was the only one to escape, he couldn't stop picturing my face when he killed them." She shook her head. "None of their families are going to get the closure they need to move on. They're still wondering what happened to their mother, their daughter or sister. They'll never know the truth."

"The FBI will keep looking," he said.

"So will I." She sniffled.

"What do you mean?" Finn pulled back, the emergency blankets crinkling loud over the consistent crash of waves against the beach. The wind had died down some, but there was still a cold aftershock sitting in his bones.

Camille looked up at him with those brilliant aquamarine eyes. "I've spent the last year trying to recover a life I wasn't sure I could ever get back. I tried to fall back in love with photography after the attack made it so I couldn't pick up my camera, but knowing those victims are still out there, that their families are still looking for them… What if my passion for photography could be used for something more? Something that can help all of those families?"

Understanding hit, and his hold on her slipped slightly. "You want to help the FBI recover the women Jeff Burnes killed but haven't found."

"I didn't see him for what he really was until it was too late, and I've held on to that guilt since the day I saw those photos on my camera." She stared out over the beach as the Florence police and his team of marshals mapped out the crime scene. "This might be my only chance to make it up to them, Finn, to bring them the closure they deserve."

She set her hand over his heart and stepped into him, fitting perfectly against him as though she'd been made specially for him. Not just physically but filling the emotional hole he'd lived with since the night he'd taken a bullet all those years ago. "Jodie Adler and all the other women he targeted deserve justice. Their families deserve to know what happened to them. I know whatever this is between us is new, and I want more than anything to find out where it's going. Because I can without a doubt tell you I've been in love with you since the moment you brought me back to life that night in my house, but I need to do this. For all of the Carver's victims who haven't been found. Whether it's assisting the FBI with their investigation or doing this on my own, I know what I have to do, and I need your help to do it."

"Then it's a good thing I know a former FBI bomb technician who can make it happen." The muscles at one corner of his mouth tugged into a smile. Finn gripped her hips in his hands. "Also, I love you, too, if that wasn't clear before, and I'm not going anywhere. No matter what happens next, you'll always be more to me than my witness."

"You'll always be my hero." Her resulting smile

lit up parts of him he hadn't felt in a long time. The Mylar blanket slipped from around her shoulders as she pressed onto her tiptoes to level her mouth with his. "So how many more boxes of brownies do you think you have stashed at the safe house?"

"WE'VE GOT ANOTHER ONE!" one of the FBI's forensic operations specialists called.

Camille wasn't sure of his name, just that he wasn't the only one of the unit tasked with finding unknown victims of the Carver who'd uncovered another body today. The dunes along the Oregon coast stretched in every direction, surrounded her, intimidated her. But with her temporary consulting and crime scene photography position and the resources of the entire FBI behind the small task force she'd convinced the director to create, she'd already been able to lead investigators to, and photograph, three burial sites.

Jeff Burnes had manipulated and perverted an FBI agent in Chicago to serve his jail time for him, using makeup and facial prosthetics to make the world believe the Carver had been captured. With the entire country buying into the lie that he'd been behind bars for the past year, the real killer had been more careful than ever to hide the victims of his obsession in order to keep up the charade as Dr.

Henry Gruner. But he hadn't been careful enough. Jeff Burnes had made a mistake. Two mistakes.

He hadn't counted on Camille surviving.

And he hadn't buried his treasure deep enough.

Casting her hand over her eyes to block out the sun, she studied the endless expanse of dunes, now turned into a shallow graveyard. The agent in charge of the task force watched as the two forensics team members a few yards to her left, at the first recovery site, brushed sand from the woman's face and neck. Another team had already cleared most of the sand from the second. Her boots sank a few inches below the surface of the sand as she closed in on the third with her new camera in hand.

After weeks of scouring missing persons reports from the area, interviewing family members and friends and visiting the homes of the women who'd been reported missing, Camille had created a working photo array of possible victim names and likenesses. Some even with photos that parents and siblings had offered to help with the search. Three bodies discovered in as many hours. Three lives ruined but never forgotten. Who knew how many more waited under a few feet of sand to be brought home?

"Who do we have here?"

The forensic specialist dug out around painted red toenails and light ankles. "Too soon to tell, but

I'll have her out in about thirty minutes for you to hopefully make a match."

"I'll start at her feet." Camille raised her camera and took the first photo of their newly recovered victim. She turned, nearly running straight into the wall of muscle who'd taken the assignment to follow her wherever this task force needed her.

"Drink up, Red." With that gut-wrenching smile in full force, Finn offered her a cold bottle of water from the collection in his arms, the condensation shocking the nerves in her heated palms. Oregon was headed into spring in the next few weeks, but the man had the ability to rocket her body temperature into dangerous territory with a single look in her direction. It'd been three weeks since he'd saved her life in that cave. Three weeks since he'd faced off with the nightmare that'd cast a shadow behind her for the past year, and during that time he'd supported her to find as many of the Carver's victims as she could to a fault. "You're looking a little flushed."

Without Finn and Deputy US Marshal Jonah Watson, she wouldn't have been able to form this task force. Without him, she wouldn't have found this new path to recover and document the victims the FBI and police couldn't or give more detailed insights into the killer they'd been investigating. Without him, she'd still be that emotionally lonely woman he'd met the day she'd been transferred into his protection detail, the one full of fear and uncertainty and scared of the idea she'd never get back what she'd lost.

"Bet you wish you were the reason." But more important, without him, she'd have to buy her own mattress chocolate and boxed brownie mix. Camille twisted off the cap of her bottle and took a drink. Cool water soothed the rawness building in her throat from the outdoor conditions and disturbance of sand, but it'd never be enough to counter her internal awareness of the marshal standing in front of her.

"Damn, I love you." He pulled her into his chest with his free hand, spilling her water across his superhero T-shirt, and lowered his mouth to hers. "If we weren't in the middle of several crime scenes, I'd show you exactly how much."

"Don't worry, Marshal Reed. You'll get your chance just as soon as we've scoured every inch of these dunes and brought these women home to their families." She smiled, happy in the knowledge she'd found the man who'd stand up to any threat that came their way, who respected her commitment and intensity to carrying out the job of this task force and would keep her laughing with their bizarre inside jokes and love of chocolate. She patted him on the shoulder and stepped back. "Until then, consider yourself nothing more than a marshal assigned to protect your witness."

She headed for the command tent feeling lighter and more certain of herself than she ever had before. With Finn's groan following her the entire way.

* * * * *

"I don't know anything," she said. "Why does TDC think
I do?"

"I don't know." Was this an especially bold gambit on
TDC's part, or merely a desperate one?

"Maybe this isn't about what TDC wants you to reveal,"
he said. "Maybe it's about what they think you know that
they don't want you to say."

She pushed her hair back from her forehead, a distracted
gesture. "I don't understand what you're getting at."

"Everything TDC is doing—the charges against your
father, the big reward, the publicity—those are the actions
of an organization that is desperate to find your father."

"Because they want to stop him from talking?"

"I could be wrong, but I think so."

Most of the color had left her face, but she remained
strong. "That sounds dangerous," she said. "A lot more
dangerous than diapers."

"You don't have any idea what TDC might be worried about?" he asked. "It could even be something your father mentioned to you in passing."

"He didn't talk to me about his work. He knew I wasn't interested."

"What did you talk about?" Maybe the answer lay there.

"What I was doing. What was going on in my life." She shrugged. "Sometimes we talked about music, or movies, or books. Travel—that was something we both enjoyed. There was nothing secret or mysterious or having anything to do with TDC."

"If you think of anything else, call me." It was what he always said to people involved in cases, but he hoped she really would call him.

"I will." Did he detect annoyance in her voice?

"What will you do about the lawsuit?" he asked.

She looked down at the white envelope. "I'll contact my attorney. The whole thing is ridiculous. And annoying." She shifted her gaze to him at the last word. Maybe a signal for him to go.

"I'll let you know if I hear any news," he said, moving toward the door.

"Thanks."

"Try not to worry," he said. Then he added, "I'll protect you." Because it was the right thing to say. Because it was his job.

Because he realized nothing was more important to him at this moment.

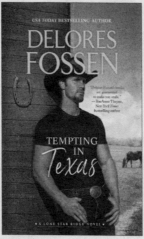

SPECIAL EXCERPT FROM

HQN

*Deputy Cait Jameson is shocked to see Hayes Dalton
back in Lone Star Ridge. What's even more surprising
is that her teen crush turned Hollywood heartthrob
has secrets he feels comfortable sharing only with her.
As they grow closer, Cait wonders just how long their
budding relationship can last before fame calls him back
and he breaks her heart all over again...*

Read on for a sneak peek at
Tempting in Texas,
*the final book in the Lone Star Ridge series
from* USA TODAY *bestselling author Delores Fossen.*

"I need to ask you for one more favor," he said. "A big
one."

"No, I'm not going to have relations with you," she
joked.

Even though he smiled a little, Cait could tell that
whatever he was about to ask would indeed be big.

"Maybe in a day or two, then." His smile faded, and
he opened his eyes, his gaze zeroing in on her. "I have
an appointment in San Antonio next week, and I was
wondering if you could take me if I'm not in any shape to
drive yet? I don't want my family to know, so that's why
I can't ask one of them," Hayes added.

She nodded cautiously. "I can take you. Are you sure you're up to a ride like that?"

"I have to be." He stared at her. "Since I know you can keep secrets, I'll tell you that it's an appointment with a psychiatrist."

Well, that got her attention.

"Okay," she said, waiting for him to tell her more.

But he didn't follow through on her suspected more. Hayes just muttered a thank-you and closed his eyes again.

Cait stood there several more moments. Still nothing from him. But she saw the rhythmic rise and fall of his chest that let her know he'd gone to sleep. Or else he was pretending to sleep so she would just leave. So that's what she did. Cait turned and left, understanding that he was putting a lot of faith in her. Then again, she was indeed good at keeping secrets.

After all, Hayes had no idea just how much she cared about him.

And if she had any say in the matter, he never would.

Don't miss
Tempting in Texas *by Delores Fossen,*
available February 2021,
wherever HQN books and ebooks are sold.

HQNBooks.com

Love Harlequin romance?

DISCOVER.

Be the first to find out about promotions,
news and exclusive content!

 Facebook.com/HarlequinBooks

Twitter.com/HarlequinBooks

Instagram.com/HarlequinBooks

Pinterest.com/HarlequinBooks

ReaderService.com

EXPLORE.

Sign up for the Harlequin e-newsletter and
download a free book from any series at
TryHarlequin.com

CONNECT.

Join our Harlequin community to
share your thoughts and connect
with other romance readers!
Facebook.com/groups/HarlequinConnection

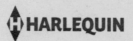

HSOCIAL2020